CHECK IT OUT— AND DIE!

Other Avon Camelot Books in the
SPINETINGLER *Series*
by M. T. Coffin

(#1) THE SUBSTITUTE CREATURE
(#2) BILLY BAKER'S DOG WON'T STAY BURIED
(#3) MY TEACHER'S A BUG
(#4) WHERE HAVE ALL THE PARENTS GONE?

Coming Soon

(#6) SIMON SAYS, "CROAK!"

SPINETINGLERS

#5

CHECK IT OUT— AND DIE!

M. T. COFFIN

AN AVON CAMELOT BOOK

CHECK IT OUT—AND DIE! is an original publication of Avon Books. This work has never before appeared in book form.

AVON BOOKS
A division of
The Hearst Corporation
1350 Avenue of the Americas
New York, New York 10019

Copyright © 1995 by George Edward Stanley
Excerpt from *Simon Says, "Croak!"* copyright © 1995 by Kathleen Duey
Published by arrangement with the author
Library of Congress Catalog Card Number: 95-90088
ISBN: 0-380-78116-6
RL: 4.9

First Avon Camelot Printing: September 1995

CAMELOT TRADEMARK REG. U.S. PAT. OFF. AND IN OTHER COUNTRIES, MARCA REGISTRADA, HECHO EN U.S.A.

Printed in the U.S.A.

OPM   10   9   8   7   6   5   4   3   2   1

CHECK IT OUT— AND DIE!

I had just passed Courtney Johnson's table, on my way to get a second carton of milk, when she screamed, "It's somebody's finger!" She pointed to her plate. There, in the middle of the mashed potatoes, was a human finger, bloody on one end, where it had obviously been severed.

"Oh, yuck!" her best friend Jean Bentley cried. "It's one of the cafeteria cook's!"

Courtney tried to push her chair away from the table, but she pushed too hard and toppled over backward.

Several boys at the next table started laughing.

"It's not funny!" Jean shouted at them. "You should see what's in the middle of her mashed potatoes!" She stood up and began helping her best friend.

The fifth graders all rushed toward Courtney's plate, but they tripped over themselves and

1

ended up on the floor before any of them could get near it.

I quickly grabbed the finger from the mashed potatoes and put it into my pocket.

"What's going on here, Stanton?" Mr. Scoville, our principal, was looking directly at me.

"Courtney fell over, and Jean's trying to help her up," I said.

Mr. Scoville looked down at Courtney, who was still lying on the floor. "Are you all right?"

"No, I am not all right," Courtney sobbed. "It was awful!"

"What was awful?" Mr. Scoville asked.

"There's a human finger in the middle of her mashed potatoes," Jean said. "It belongs to one of the cafeteria cooks!"

Mr. Scoville looked stunned. *"What?"* He turned around and looked at Courtney's plate with disgust. Then he took a fork and stirred the mashed potatoes. "I don't see anything in here."

I decided it was time to return to my own table. While Mr. Scoville was digging around in the mashed potatoes some more, I began walking away. I knew I had to slip the rubber finger to someone else before Mr. Scoville got suspicious and decided to search me.

I finally reached my table, two over from Courtney's, and showed the finger to Dustin Montgomery. "Hide this in your pocket."

"Where'd you get *that*?" Dustin demanded.

"It's a long story."

"It has mashed potatoes on it, Charlie! Wipe it off!"

I took my napkin, wiped off the finger under the table, so no one would see me and tell Mr. Scoville, then I handed it to Dustin, who quickly put it inside his pocket.

"Charlie Stanton!"

I was sure I jumped two feet out of my seat. Mr. Scoville was standing right behind me.

"Yes, sir?"

"Stand up and empty your pockets!"

"Okay." I stood up and emptied my pockets. Two pieces of candy fell out. I gave Mr. Scoville a puzzled look.

"I know you're behind this, Stanton, but I can't prove it. Right before a full moon, someone always starts putting rubber body parts in people's food, and I think that someone is you!" Then Mr. Scoville turned around and stormed out of the cafeteria.

Several of the kids around us started snickering.

"That was really close," Dustin said. "Want your finger back now?"

3

"No, you'd better keep it for a while. Mr. Scoville may decide to search me again. Anyway, it's not my finger."

"What do you mean, it's not your finger?"

"I think it belongs to that new girl, Davina Dishman. I saw her drop something onto Courtney's plate when Courtney wasn't looking."

Dustin and I looked around the cafeteria until we spotted Davina. She was sitting over in a corner by herself.

"You mean there's someone else in this school besides you who likes to play practical jokes with body parts, and it's a *girl*?"

"Yeah. Isn't it great? I wonder if she likes to read horror books, too."

"A lot of us like to read horror books, Charlie, but you're the only one who acts them out!"

"Until now, you mean."

Dustin looked at his watch. "It's almost time for class. Come on."

I followed Dustin to the rear of the cafeteria to put our trays on the conveyer belt.

I tried to make eye contact with Davina Dishman to let her know she had a friend at Edison Elementary School, but she kept looking at the food on her plate. I even thought about going over to tell her how glad I was to have her here, but I decided this might not be the best time to intro-

4

duce myself, so I followed Dustin out of the cafeteria.

Courtney and Jean were waiting for us just outside the door.

"You creep!" Courtney shouted at me. "You're totally disgusting!"

"What are you talking about, Courtney?"

"You know precisely what I'm talking about, Charlie Stanton. You put that awful disgusting finger in my mashed potatoes! Where'd you get it?"

"Did you dig up somebody's grave and break it off?" Jean asked sarcastically.

"No, but that's a really great idea, Jean! Thanks for suggesting it!"

Courtney and Jean shuddered and hurried away.

"You can't even take a little joke!" Dustin called to them.

"Well, we can cross them off the list," I said. I pulled a list out of my pocket and crossed off two names.

"What's that?" Dustin asked.

"I made a list last night of all the kids I thought might be interested in joining a horror club."

"What do you mean, a 'horror club'? I've never heard of such a thing."

5

"There's one in this book I'm reading. If we had a horror club, we'd get together on Friday nights at someone's house and watch horror movies or read horror books. We could even make up our own horror stories, where we'd be the characters."

"That's a great idea. Did you put Davina Dishman's name on the list?"

"I'm doing that as we speak."

Dustin sighed. "I wish we could read horror books during library period."

"Yeah, but Mrs. Hart would never let us do that." I was remembering all the times I'd tried and all the times I'd been caught and had my books confiscated or had been sent to the principal's office. "Mr. Scoville still has two of my favorite books, *The Body in My Backpack* and *Body Parts for Lunch*. I need to get them back."

"Yeah, I liked those, too. Hey, that's where Davina got the idea of putting a finger in Courtney's mashed potatoes, isn't it?"

I nodded. "Except in *Body Parts for Lunch,* it was a *real* finger."

"I remember. It was great! Oh, hey, I want to stop by my locker first and get my book, so I'll have it with me for last hour."

Dustin's locker was just around the corner from the cafeteria.

"Let me see if I can remember your combination," I said.

"It's not locked. It's broken. They keep telling me they're going to fix it, but they haven't done anything yet."

"They probably won't, either. My dad said they don't want to spend any more money on this old building."

Dustin yanked the door open and a bloody body fell out. He screamed, grabbed at it, and fell backward.

"Hey, everybody! Look!" I cried. "There's a dead person in Dustin's locker!"

Other kids came running down the hall.

Several teachers started pushing their way through the throng.

Everyone was shouting, "Who is it? Who is it? Do you know him? Do you know him?"

Dustin was now on the floor, trying frantically to free himself from the body that had fallen on top of him. "Help me!" he cried. "Help me!"

I wanted to help him, but he looked so funny I couldn't stop laughing long enough to do anything.

Everyone else was now laughing hysterically, too.

Finally, Mr. Scoville appeared. He looked right at me and said, "What's going on here, Stanton?"

It took me a minute to catch my breath. "Well, when Dustin opened his locker, this dead dummy fell out on top of him," I said, trying to keep a straight face, "and now he's all covered with red stuff, and—"

"*Dead* dummy?" Mr. Scoville screamed. He looked down at Dustin with disgust. Suddenly, he yanked the dummy off and slung it down the hall, covering everyone with the red stuff.

"It's *ketchup*!" someone shouted.

"My new shirt!"

"My new dress!"

"It's awful!"

"What a mess!" one of the teachers cried.

"Everyone to fourth hour!" Mr. Scoville shouted. "Now! Go! I mean *everyone*!"

The students who were covered with ketchup headed to the rest rooms. The teachers headed to the teachers' lounge.

With my help, Dustin was finally able to stand up. "Come on," I said to him, "let's go get cleaned up."

"Not so fast!" Mr. Scoville said.

We looked up into his scowling face. "This is it! You've had it!" he screamed. "Go wash all that ketchup off and then report to my office!"

"Yes, sir," we said in unison.

We turned and headed toward the nearest rest

8

room. When we got there, no one else was around, but there were plenty of red-stained paper towels in the trash can.

"Can you believe Mr. Scoville actually thinks we put that stupid dummy in my locker for a joke?" Dustin said. He looked at himself in the mirror. "Oh, man, this is a brand-new shirt. My mother's going to kill me if this ketchup doesn't come out!" He turned back to me. "Who could have done it, Charlie?"

"It had to be Davina Dishman. I just know it was."

"You really think so?"

"Yes, and I need to talk to her, too. If she keeps this up, she's going to ruin all the things I've worked so hard to achieve!"

It took us about ten minutes to get all the ketchup off our clothes, then we reluctantly left the rest room, turned the corner, and headed toward the principal's office.

Mrs. Penn, the secretary, was at her desk, but Mr. Scoville was nowhere around.

We sat down on the hard bench that everybody sits on when they've been called to the office.

"Do you have an appointment, gentlemen?" Mrs. Penn asked.

I nodded. "Mr. Scoville wants to see us."

"Well, he's on the telephone now with another

problem that just came up, poor man." Mrs. Penn looked at her watch. "I think it may be quite a while, too."

So we waited an hour and a half.

Finally, I said, "We're going to miss library period, Mrs. Penn."

"I like library period," Dustin added.

Mrs. Penn gave us her best motherly look. "Why don't we do it this way, then? You both go on to your library period. I'll tell Mr. Scoville you came by as requested. I'll come get you if he needs to see you today. I honestly believe, however, that it might have to wait until Monday."

Oh, great, I thought. Now I'll worry about it all weekend. I sighed. "Okay." Dustin and I stood up. "Thanks, Mrs. Penn."

She smiled. "Good luck!"

Mrs. Penn was one of the nicest people I knew. She didn't even get mad the time I put all those plastic eyeballs on her desk.

We left the principal's office, headed back down the hall, entered the library, and stopped immediately.

Sitting behind the desk was a woman we'd never seen before.

"A *substitute*?" Dustin whispered.

"I hope so. Maybe she won't care what we read.

10

I've been wanting to finish *Who's Buried in the Basement?*"

We took a seat at one of the tables in the first row. It was the only table that had two empty chairs together. Dustin and I usually sat in the back, so we could try to read our horror books without getting caught.

The woman was writing something in a notebook. Finally, she looked out over the room and said, "I'm Ms. Gunkel. I'll be the librarian for the next few weeks. Mrs. Hart is ill."

Dustin turned to me and grinned.

"Look!" I whispered to him. I pointed to a canvas tote bag on the table. I was sure I could see some Stephen King novels sticking out of it. My heart skipped a beat. Did Ms. Gunkel actually read horror books? I wondered. That would be almost too much to hope for. It was one thing to tolerate them. It was something entirely different if she actually read them.

I raised my hand.

"Yes?"

"My name's Charlie Stanton, and, well, I was just wondering, do you like to read horror books?"

"I read them all the time. They're my favorites!"

"Do you mind if we read them during library period?"

"Oh, no. Actually, I *encourage* it."

Dustin and I looked at each other and grinned again. I couldn't believe what I was hearing.

"Do you like horror books, Charlie?" Ms. Gunkel asked.

"I read them all the time, too," I announced proudly.

"So do I!" Dustin chimed in.

"So do I!" said a voice at the back of the room.

Dustin and I turned. Davina Dishman was sitting at a table in the rear. She had a big grin on her face.

"In fact," Ms. Gunkel continued, "I plan to start a horror reading club."

My heart was beating big time.

"I invite any of you who are interested in joining this club to stay just a minute after school and I'll tell you all about the plans I have for you!"

"I'll stay!" I cried.

Right after I said it, though, I had the strangest feeling I might live to regret it.

2

"I wonder what Ms. Gunkel has in mind," Dustin said excitedly.

We had both gone to the office to call our parents and tell them we wouldn't be home right after school because we were staying for an important meeting, but the lines were busy.

"Who knows? Who cares? I still can't believe it!"

Davina Dishman was going back into the library ahead of us.

"Davina!" I called.

She turned. Dustin and I introduced ourselves.

"That was great," I said.

"What are you talking about?"

"The finger in the mashed potatoes. The bloody body in the locker. You're a credit to horror readers everywhere."

Davina looked around to see if anyone else was

listening to us. "I did the finger, but I didn't do the body," she whispered. "Ms. Gunkel did that."

I was sure my mouth dropped almost to the floor. "Come on, Davina. No teacher is going to play a horror practical joke like that on a kid."

"I saw her. Anyway, if I just admitted to you that I put the severed finger in the mashed potatoes, then why wouldn't I admit that I put the dead body in Dustin's locker?" She sighed. "I just wish I had thought of it. That was prime horror!"

"I think she's telling the truth, Charlie," Dustin said. "Why wouldn't she take credit for it if she had done it?"

"I see your point." I thought for a minute. This was getting more and more interesting. Not only did the new librarian read horror, she acted it out. "Come on. I want to find out everything about Ms. Gunkel's horror reading club. Hers may be more fun than the one I had in mind."

The library was packed when we got there. Most of the kids were just standing around, but Trudy Jones was sitting in a chair at the front of the room, near the librarian's desk. There were three empty chairs next to her. I motioned for Dustin and Davina to follow me.

I introduced Davina to Trudy. "She put the finger in Courtney Johnson's mashed potatoes."

"I'm impressed," Trudy said. "Did you do the bloody body in Dustin's locker, too?"

Davina shook her head.

"Ms. Gunkel did that," Dustin said.

Trudy blinked. "Please. A teacher who plays practical horror jokes? Give me a break."

"I saw her," Davina insisted.

I nodded. "It's beginning to make sense."

Trudy smiled. "Well, well, well. This little meeting may turn out to be more interesting than I thought it would." She looked at us. "Why are you all still standing? I saved these three seats for you."

Sometimes Trudy spooked me. She seemed to have a second sense about her. I'm sure she knew Dustin and I would be there, but how did she know about Davina?

The three of us sat down just as Ms. Gunkel came into the main room from one of the storage areas. She sat down on the corner of the desk and smiled at everyone, but I was sure she gave the four of us her biggest smile.

"Young people like to read horror," she began.

It was a statement, not a question, but we all nodded our heads in agreement.

"I have a wonderful collection of horror books which I'm going to donate temporarily to the Edison Elementary School library, but I need some help in getting them from the basement of my house to my van and then over here to the library."

"I'll help!" I said.

"Good." Ms. Gunkel paused and looked over the room. "I was hoping you'd all help in some way. I'll also need people to catalog them and put them on the shelves because I want them ready to be checked out Monday morning. That's very important."

The crowd stirred. Several more kids volunteered, "I'll help! I'll help!"

It was quite obvious to Ms. Gunkel that we could hardly wait.

Ms. Gunkel scanned the crowd again until her eyes finally rested on the four of us in front. "Can you be at my house tonight to help me carry the books up from my basement and then put them into my van?"

We nodded. I felt mesmerized.

"I'll want to bring them to the library tonight. Can you also help do that?"

The four of us nodded again.

"We'll unbox them and get them ready to be cataloged on Saturday? Can you help do that?"

We nodded a third time.

"Good!" Ms. Gunkel cried. She clapped her hands together.

I blinked. I felt as though I had been asleep. Beside me, Dustin yawned.

Ms. Gunkel smiled. "How many of the rest of you can be here all day Saturday to help me get the books ready for the shelves?"

Everyone in the room raised a hand. This was incredible, I thought. Here were all of these kids ready to give up their Saturday to work in the school library. I mean, it was like Ms. Gunkel had a hold on them or something, but that was ridiculous. I knew the only reason was that they all liked to read horror books just like me. Especially a first-class collection like Ms. Gunkel was sure to have.

"Fine," Ms. Gunkel said. She turned back to the four of us. "My address is Twenty Owl Lane. It's the last house before the cemetery. I'll see you tonight at eight o'clock."

Dustin looked at me, rolled his eyes, and grinned. "The *cemetery*? This gets better and better."

"Yes, it does," I agreed.

When Ms. Gunkel dismissed us, I went up to her desk and whispered, "That was a great practical joke you played on Dustin, putting that dummy covered with ketchup in his locker. I was really impressed."

"You liked that, did you?" Ms. Gunkel's eyes

17

seemed to bore into me. "Well, that's good, Charlie, because I've got even more tricks up my sleeve."

I wanted to ask her what they were, but somebody else came up and asked Ms. Gunkel a question.

I walked home with Dustin and we made arrangements for him to spend the night with me.

Trudy did the same with Davina.

Then we almost hit a snag.

It wasn't that my parents minded our helping out a teacher, it was that it just seemed strange to them that she wanted us to do it so late on a Friday night.

"Couldn't she wait until in the morning?" Dad asked when he was still trying to decide if Dustin and I could go or not.

"She has this all worked out to the last minute," I explained. "She wants to make sure the books are on the shelves in the library so that kids can start checking them out on Monday morning."

"Well, I think they should be allowed to go," Mom said. "I think it's wonderful that a teacher today is willing to go to that much trouble to get kids to read."

Dustin and I agreed with her.

Finally, Dad said it was all right.

18

At seven-thirty, Trudy and Davina arrived at our house, so we could all walk over to Ms. Gunkel's house together.

"Did your parents think this was weird?" Trudy asked me as we started down the street.

"Yes. Did yours?"

Trudy nodded.

The town we live in, Duncanville, isn't very large, so it doesn't take too long to get almost anywhere. Owl Street is two blocks south of my street. From there, it's about eight blocks to the cemetery.

"Why are so many of these streetlights out?" Trudy asked.

I had thought it was darker than usual, but I hadn't thought about the reason why. "I don't know." I suddenly wondered if it was an omen or something.

"I see the cemetery up ahead," Dustin said.

Owl Street dead-ended at the iron gates to the Duncanville Cemetery, so I knew we were almost to Ms. Gunkel's house. For some reason, my heart had begun to pound wildly.

When we finally reached it, it was exactly what I had expected: a two-story wooden house that looked haunted. It was funny, but I didn't remember ever having noticed it before. Of course,

I hardly ever came down this dead-end street, so I wouldn't have passed it often.

"It's perfect," Davina said.

"What do you mean, perfect?" Dustin asked.

"It's just the right setting for a horror reading club. Maybe Ms. Gunkel will let us come over here some evening and talk about the horror books we're reading. Maybe we can even act them out, you know, like play monster hide-and-seek."

"What's monster hide-and-seek?" I asked.

"It's sort of like regular hide-and-seek except that someone is the monster in the latest horror book that everyone's reading. You turn off all the lights and hide and let the monster try to find you. It's great. I mean, it's just like being in a horror movie. We played it at my old school."

"Sounds like fun," Trudy said.

I thought it did, too, except I wanted to take this one step at a time. What I wanted to do first was find out what kind of horror books Ms. Gunkel was planning to put in the library. "I hope these books of hers are really scary."

"I do, too," Dustin agreed. "I don't want any of that kid stuff with the green slime!"

"Well, we'll soon find out," Trudy said. She hurried up the steep porch steps and knocked.

We followed her.

It took several minutes for Ms. Gunkel to open

the door, but when she did, we were all really surprised.

"Wow!" Dustin said. He was looking past Ms. Gunkel into the front room of the house.

I couldn't believe what I was seeing, either. There were hundreds of burning candles.

"The electric company hasn't turned on the electricity yet, so I'm using candles until they do."

"This is awesome!" I said.

"Well, come on in, and let's get started," Ms. Gunkel said. She stepped away from the door.

The four of us slowly walked into the front room. It was unbelievable.

"I've never seen so many candles in all my life," Trudy said. "It's just like a scene from . . ."

"The Candles of Death," Davina said, finishing her sentence.

"Exactly," Ms. Gunkel replied. "I am impressed with your knowledge of horror books."

Then I saw a coffin in a corner of the room and froze. "What's . . . *that?*"

Ms. Gunkel smiled. "Why don't you go find out, Charlie?"

"Me?"

Ms. Gunkel nodded.

"Oh, I'm not sure I really want to do that, Ms. Gunkel."

"I'll do it, then," Dustin said.

"No, I'll do it," I said hurriedly. "She asked me first." I wasn't going to let Dustin show me up.

I walked over to the coffin. There were candelabra on both sides of it, which seemed to make it shimmer.

I slowly reached out to open the lid.

Ms. Gunkel screamed.

I jumped three feet into the air, I was sure. "What's wrong?" I cried.

"A bat! I hate bats!"

Flying around the room was a black object that seemed to be going crazy.

Dustin held the front door open and it flew out.

"Where'd it come from?" Trudy asked.

"The basement is full of them," Ms. Gunkel replied.

"The *basement*?" I said. "Isn't that where the books are?"

"Yes. Most of them," Ms. Gunkel replied.

I had suddenly decided this might not be so much fun after all, but I knew we couldn't stop now. The rest of the kids at school were counting on us.

I found the side latch on the coffin, pressed it, and then slowly started to raise the lid.

"Stop!" Ms. Gunkel screamed. "Don't open it!"

"What's wrong?" Trudy cried. "What's in it?"

"Books," Ms. Gunkel replied.

"Books?" we all cried in unison.

"Yes." Ms. Gunkel started laughing. "You passed the test, Charlie."

"What test?"

"You had no idea what was in that coffin and yet you weren't afraid to open it up."

She didn't know the half of it, I thought. "You mean all the books you're going to put in the library are in here in this coffin?"

"Oh, no, no, there are hundreds and hundreds more down in the basement. In fact, I may not even take what's in that coffin."

"Are the other books inside coffins, too?" Dustin asked.

"Yes."

"Why?" Trudy asked.

"They make wonderful trunks for shipping things, that's why. Absolutely no one will open them up to steal anything."

"Is that why you bought them?" Davina asked.

"Oh, no, I didn't buy them, dear. They all belonged to my late husband. He owned a funeral home in Indiana. When he died, the coffins were the only things left after I paid our bills, so I just kept them and started storing things in them. When I decided to move out here, instead of using cardboard boxes, I just moved everything like this."

23

Wow! I thought. I had never met anyone like Ms. Gunkel.

She clapped her hands. "Well, if we're going to get all of these books to the library, then we'd better get started. This way, everyone!"

Ms. Gunkel led us out of the front room into the kitchen and through a door that led down to the basement.

When we got to the bottom of the steps, there was a really terrible smell. That creepy feeling I had had earlier was coming back.

Everywhere there were hundreds and hundreds of candles burning, and, just as Ms. Gunkel had said, too, the basement was full of coffins and the coffins were full of books.

We put them into paper grocery sacks and began carrying them up the stairs, through the kitchen and the front room, out the front door, and down the porch steps to the side of the house, where Ms. Gunkel's van was waiting.

It took us about an hour.

Then we all squeezed into the van and rode with Ms. Gunkel to the school, where it started all over again, only in reverse.

We took the bags of books into the library and stacked them on the tables, so they could be cataloged tomorrow.

"This is the first time I've ever been in the school this late at night," Trudy said.

"This is another great place to play monster hide-and-seek," Davina said.

"You have some great ideas, Davina," I said. I was already thinking about suggesting to Ms. Gunkel that Davina be put in charge of the parties when we started the horror reading club.

"Well, that's it," Ms. Gunkel said. "They're all ready for the students to work on tomorrow."

"Need any more help?" Trudy asked.

"I don't think so," Ms. Gunkel replied. "You've helped me enough already."

With that, we all piled back into the van and Ms. Gunkel drove back to her house. I started once to suggest that she drop us all off at my house, but for some reason I didn't.

We said our good-byes and started walking away, but when we got to the street, I looked back once and, through one of the windows, I was sure I saw someone getting out of that coffin in the front room.

I didn't say anything about it then because I didn't want to believe there was more to what Ms. Gunkel was doing than what she had said there was, but after thinking about it all weekend, I finally mentioned it to Dustin Monday morning at school.

He convinced me that my eyes had been playing tricks on me because of all the flickering candles.

"Yeah, that's probably it." I sighed. "I can hardly wait until library period!"

All morning we had to listen to other kids talking about what great horror books they'd checked out of the library.

"There won't be any left by the time we get there," Dustin said. "Why do we have to have library period last hour?"

"Don't worry about it. They can't check them

all out," I said. "Don't you remember how many books there were?"

"I remember, but there were only a few that I really wanted to read, and they're probably all gone by now."

Actually, I felt the same way. I was just hoping the ones I wanted would still be there, too.

Finally, it was our turn.

The new horror books were all in a huge special shelf at the back of the library. I didn't remember ever having seen that shelf before. Ms. Gunkel had probably put it up herself on Sunday afternoon, I decided. It was now about half empty.

"Sleepover!" I said to Dustin. "It's still there."

"I saw that, too. It looks good."

"What are you going to get?"

"The main one I wanted is already checked out. I just knew it would be. It was called *Rats in My Bedroom.*" He looked over several of the remaining titles. "I think I'll read this. *School Trip.*"

"I think I'll read that one after you. Come on. Let's get these and check them out."

When we got to Ms. Gunkel's desk, she took the books, put them under a special light, we heard a beep, and then she said, "Well, you're all set. You may now start reading."

Dustin and I hurried to the back of the room. I could see that Trudy and Davina already had their books, but instead of reading them, they were talking excitedly about something.

Dustin and I sat down and started reading.

I was halfway through the first page when I heard someone snoring. I looked up, ready to tell them to be quiet, when I realized I wasn't even in the library anymore. I was in the living room of a house I'd never seen before.

"What happened? Dustin? Where are you?"

I stood up. What in the world was going on here? I wondered. "Hey! Is there anybody here?"

Suddenly another boy appeared at a doorway. He was dressed in pajamas and was yawning. I had never seen him before. "What are you doing, Bobby?"

"My name's not Bobby," I said. "My name's Charlie Stanton."

The boy just looked at me. "You have to be quieter, Bobby, or you'll wake up my parents." He yawned again. "It's late. Why don't you come on to bed?"

Why did he keep calling me Bobby? I wondered. I looked around. "How'd I get here?" Somewhere in the distance I could still hear the snoring sound. "Who's that?"

"It's Dad, and if you wake him up, he'll be mad

28

because he didn't want me having company anyway." He took me by the arm.

Why, I don't know, but I let him lead me toward the dark hallway he'd just come down.

We passed a room the snoring was coming from. I gasped when I looked through the door.

"What's going on here?" I whispered. Inside the room, a man and a woman were lying in open coffins. The man was snoring. I looked at this boy I had never seen before. "Are you people vampires or what?"

The boy laughed. "Of course not, Bobby. My family just sleeps in coffins. They're very comfortable."

I tried to pull away from him, but he held me so tightly I couldn't.

He continued leading me toward a room at the end of the hall.

"Let me go!" I shouted at him. "Let me go!"

"Quiet! You'll wake up Dad," the boy hissed at me. "He'll be really angry if you do."

"Where are you taking me?"

"You have to go to bed, Bobby. It's time to go to bed."

"My name's Charlie, and I'm not sleepy! Couldn't I stay up and watch television or something?"

"No."

"But I don't want to go to bed!" I shouted.

We had reached the room at the end of the hall. A night-light was on and I could see a coffin on each side of the room.

"Your coffin is all ready, Bobby," the boy said. "Just climb in and go to sleep."

"No! I don't want to sleep in a coffin!"

"They're very comfortable, Bobby. Come on, now!"

I gave one final tug and pulled loose from his grip. Then I turned around and raced back down the hall.

"Bobby!" the boy cried. The sound of his voice sent chills through me.

I reached the room where I had first realized I was no longer in the library. I ran to what I was sure was the front door. It was locked. I managed to turn the dead bolt and take off the chain, but the screen door was locked, too.

"Bobby!" the boy cried.

"My name's not Bobby," I said as I frantically tried to get the screen door unlocked, "and I'm not going to sleep in any coffin!"

I finally got the door unlocked just as the boy came into the room.

I was out the door, down the steps, onto the sidewalk, and into the street in just a few seconds. I looked over my shoulder to see if the boy

30

was chasing me. He wasn't, but I didn't slow down.

I ran down the center of the street.

It looked like a normal street in a normal town, but I had no idea where it was.

I kept running.

I ran through a red light.

I ran by a school building.

I stopped. There was a sign in front of me:

PARKERVILLE ELEMENTARY SCHOOL

How could this be? I wondered.

Parkerville was the name of the fictional town in the book I was reading called *Sleepover!* Then I remembered that Bobby was the name of the main character, too.

My heart skipped a beat. I was *living* the book!

I hadn't gotten far enough along in it to know what else happened, but Bobby must have discovered that the friend he was spending the night with slept in coffins! How did he survive? I wondered. How did the book end?

"Bobby! You can't get away!" a voice echoed in the street. "You'll have to go to sleep sooner or later!"

"That's what you think!" I muttered under my breath. Then I started running again.

There had to be a way out of this town, didn't there, even if it was a *fictional* town? I had to be

31

wrong about all of this! There was no way I could be living a story in a book. Things like that just didn't happen.

I turned the corner at the end of the block and found myself on another pretty tree-lined street.

I kept running.

Finally, I was so tired I had to slow down. So far, I hadn't seen anyone else. Of course, I really didn't know what time it was, either, except that it was dark. Most people were probably in bed.

Then it hit me. I could find a policeman. I could tell him what had happened and he'd show me how to get out of this town and back to where I belonged.

I stopped.

Up ahead I had seen a van pull into the driveway of a house. I hid behind one of the big trees lining the street and waited to see what would happen. Finally, a woman got out.

My heart almost stopped! It was Ms. Gunkel!

"Ms. Gunkel!" I cried. I started running toward her. "Ms. Gunkel!"

Ms. Gunkel stopped and turned toward the direction of my voice.

When I finally reached her, I was so out of breath, all I could do was heave.

"What do you want, Charlie?" she asked.

"What's happening to me?" I finally managed

to say. I had suddenly realized that I was standing in front of a house that looked exactly like Ms. Gunkel's house in Duncanville. "I was in the library reading *Sleepover!* and then all of a sudden I was in this kid's house, and he was wanting me to spend the night in a coffin!"

Ms. Gunkel shrugged. "You chose the book you wanted to read, Charlie. No one else did. Now you'll just have to finish it."

"I want to go home, Ms. Gunkel. I want to go to sleep in my own bed!"

"I'm afraid that's not possible, Charlie." She looked at her watch. "I have to go. I have so much to do. There are a lot of other books I want to put on the shelves of the library."

"Bobby!"

I turned and was looking up into the face of the kid in my horror book. "Get away from me! My name's not Bobby!"

He slowly held out his hand. "Come on, Bobby. You woke up Dad, and he's really angry about it, too. You're the one who wanted to spend the night at my house, and now you're acting crazy. My parents may not let you come over again if you don't go back with me."

"I don't want to spend the night with you!" I screamed. Then I started running back in the direction I had come.

When I got to the corner of Parkerville Elementary School I turned and ran the opposite direction from the boy's house. This town looked so pleasant on the outside, but it was a horror story on the inside.

Up ahead I thought I could see brighter streetlights. I slowed down, not knowing what I was going to find. Suddenly I was in the town square.

All of the businesses were closed, except one, a small café. I put my hand in my pocket and pulled out what money I had. I counted it quickly. It came to exactly one dollar. I was sure that would buy me something. I was suddenly starving to death.

I walked slowly past the café, glanced in quickly and saw that there were about three other people in it, then I continued to the end of the block, where I turned around and headed back toward the front door.

When I opened it, a bell jangled, startling me and causing everyone to look up.

I stopped.

I was ready to run back out into the street if anyone moved, but they all returned to what they were doing, eating and talking.

I sat down at the counter. The woman behind it smiled and said, "You're out kind of late, aren't you?"

I nodded. "We just got in from visiting sick relatives, but there was nothing in the house to eat, so my dad said I could come down here and get something."

"Well, what'll you have, then?" she said.

I was amazed at how quickly the story had come out of my mouth.

"I just have a dollar," I said.

She looked at me and then looked around to see if anyone else was listening. "Well, I'll tell you what. I have one more piece of that chocolate pie over there and I don't think it'll sell tonight and it won't be good tomorrow, so I'll give you that and a big glass of milk for a dollar. Interested?"

"Yeah, sure," I said, grinning. I was thinking maybe the nightmare was over.

She put the pie and milk in front of me, and I handed her the dollar.

"I've got a boy your age at home. Do you know him? Freddie Collins?"

I shook my head.

"What's your name?"

"Charlie Stanton."

"Stanton. Stanton." She seemed to be thinking and I was beginning to get nervous. "I don't remember any Stantons in town and I thought I knew everybody."

I held my breath.

35

She smiled again. "Well, that shows you what I know."

I let my breath out and relaxed.

When I finished, I made a decision. She seemed like a really nice lady and she had a son my age, so she'd probably understand. "Look, I wasn't telling the truth. I don't really live here. In fact, I don't know how I even got here, but if I could just find some place to stay until morning, I think I'd be all right."

"You poor kid. Of course you can stay with us." She looked at her watch. "It's time I closed up this place anyway and went home."

She shooed the remaining customers out, locked up something in a safe, and turned off the lights. "I'll take care of the rest of this in the morning."

I followed her out the front door.

She locked it and said, "I just live a couple of blocks from here. Come on."

"I really appreciate this," I said.

She smiled but didn't say anything else.

We walked the two blocks in silence.

When we finally reached her house, she unlocked the front door and I followed her inside.

She turned on a small table lamp.

"I can just sleep here on the couch. It'll be all right," I said.

36

"Oh, no, I wouldn't think of that. My son has an extra coffin in his room."

"Coffin?" I screamed.

Then I blinked.

I was back in the library at Edison Elementary School, and Trudy was standing beside my table.

"I'm sorry, Charlie. I hope I didn't lose your place." She gave me a puzzled look. "Where were you anyway?"

I shook my head to clear it. "What are you talking about?"

"I came over to talk to you, but you weren't here. When I turned to leave, I knocked your book off the table and it fell shut. I bent down to pick it up and then all of a sudden you were sitting here again. I hope I didn't lose your place."

I stood up. "It's all right. I was just about . . ." I stopped. I didn't feel like explaining what had happened. It had to have been a dream, but it certainly didn't feel like one. "Where's Dustin?"

"I don't know. I guess he left and went outside. Davina did. I didn't see him leave, though. I was talking to Ms. Gunkel."

I looked at her. "Did you and Davina read your books?"

Trudy shook her head. "We got too busy talk-

37

ing. I'm saving mine for tonight when it's late. So's Davina."

I looked around the room. There were still several kids in the library, but there didn't seem to be as many as there had been at the beginning of library period. I looked at my watch. It was almost time for school to be over, so maybe Dustin had gone outside after all. Sometimes we were allowed to do that if we had finished reading.

I saw Ms. Gunkel at the front of the room. She was writing something in that notebook of hers. I thought about going up and telling her what had happened, but something kept me from doing it.

"Are you all right, Charlie?" Trudy asked.

I thought for a minute. "I'm not sure," I said. "I'm just not sure."

Then the bell to dismiss school rang.

4

I finally decided that I had had a really weird daydream. Either that or I'd fallen asleep at the table. There couldn't be any other explanation. To prove it, though, I needed to find Dustin. He'd probably laugh about it when I told him.

Trudy said she needed to talk to her music teacher before she left school, so I told her I'd call her later.

I left the library without Ms. Gunkel's saying anything. I didn't even look back to see if she was watching me leave.

Dustin wasn't on the school grounds waiting for me, like he usually did if we didn't leave the library together. Where would he have gone? I wondered. I couldn't believe he had just walked home by himself.

I suddenly remembered the book he had been reading. *School Trip*. Was that where he was now? On a *school trip*, like I had been on a *sleepover*?

No! It couldn't be! He had started reading the book, stopped for some reason, and then just left.

Why hadn't he said something to me, though?

Maybe he couldn't have, I realized. Maybe I had disappeared into my book while he was reading his. Did he think I had just left? Why would he think that, though? We were only allowed to go outside if there were just a few minutes left of library period, not right after we had started reading! Anyway, I would have said something to Dustin. He'd know that. None of this was making any sense.

I didn't really want to consider the obvious, that the same thing had happened to Dustin that had happened to me, that at this very moment he was *living* the horror book he was reading.

Then I suddenly remembered something else. His book hadn't been on the table like mine had been. Of course! That meant he had it with him!

Trudy had knocked my book onto the floor, closing it, then while she was bending down to pick it up, I was suddenly back in the library, sitting in my chair at the table. Was it my book that had brought me back? I wondered. It was all so crazy!

I had to find Dustin!

When I was almost to his house, though, I stopped and stood by the huge maple tree we'd often climbed and thought about what I was going to say to his parents. I finally decided I'd just say Dustin left school before I did because I had to make up an assignment or something like that and I was wondering if he was home yet.

Of course, that'd worry them, but I'd tell them he'd probably be along any minute, that he might have stayed for a meeting to organize a soccer team. He'd been talking about doing it anyway.

With that decided, I started toward Dustin's house again.

His mother answered the door on the first ring. "Hi, Charlie." When she saw I was the only one standing on the front porch, she said, "Where's Dustin?"

"Oh, I don't guess he's home then. I just thought his meeting might be over."

His mother looked puzzled. "What meeting?"

"Uh, well, he said something about a soccer meeting, so I guess he stayed for it after all. I had something else to do, so we didn't walk home together. Will you have him call me when he gets in?"

"Sure, Charlie. By any chance, do you know how long the meeting will be?"

I swallowed. "You know something. Now that

41

I think of it, it might be late because I think they were also going to have a practice after the meeting."

Mrs. Montgomery shook her head. "Well, when he gets home, we're certainly going to have a talk because he didn't say anything about this. If you hadn't come by, I wouldn't have known where he was."

The last thing I wanted to do was cause Dustin more trouble, so I said, "Well, I'm not quite sure he even knew about it, Mrs. Montgomery. I think they just announced it at school this morning."

Mrs. Montgomery sighed. "He could have at least telephoned."

I started to say that he might not have had time, but I thought I had probably pushed it far enough as it was.

"Maybe I'll call him later myself," I said, heading down the steps of the porch. "Would you tell him I came by?"

"All right, Charlie. We'll see you later."

I started running.

I knew now that Dustin had disappeared, but it wasn't anywhere in Duncanville. He had disappeared into his horror book, *School Trip*.

I thought about going back to the library and confronting Ms. Gunkel, but I was sure that somehow she was responsible for all of this and wouldn't be interested in helping me find Dustin. In fact, she was probably angry that I had made it back myself.

But what was the secret? How could I have made it back and not Dustin? Why was my book still on the table and not his?

I had to get home fast and think up some way to get Dustin back home.

When I got there, I found Mom in her workroom. She designs cross-stitch patterns, which sell very well all over the country.

"I'm hungry," I said. "Is there anything to eat?" I always think better with a full stomach.

"There's some cake on the table, Charlie, but just one piece, okay, because when your dad gets home and gets cleaned up we're going out for Mexican food."

"Couldn't we just eat here at home tonight, Mom?"

She frowned at me. "It's your favorite restaurant, Charlie. Zapata's."

"But I've got a lot of homework."

Mom raised an eyebrow. "That's never stopped you before. You want to invite Dustin to go along?"

"No!"

She stood up. "Charlie? What's wrong with you? Did you and Dustin have a fight?"

"No, Mom. It's just that . . . well, it wasn't a very good day."

"You were so excited this morning because of that new librarian. Did you get out any new horror books?"

"Yes." I didn't want to talk about this anymore. "I'm sorry. I guess I'll have time to go eat after all."

"Well, do you want to invite Dustin or not?"

"He's busy. We can take him next time."

Mom shrugged. "Okay."

I went into the kitchen, cut myself a big piece of cake, and poured myself a big glass of milk. Then I sat down to think.

I knew Dustin had disappeared where no one except me and Ms. Gunkel would believe. I had to do something to get him back, but I needed help. There were only two other people I thought I could trust at this point: Trudy and Davina.

I knew Trudy's telephone number, but I didn't know Davina's. I had a feeling, though, that Davina would be at Trudy's house. I looked at my watch. It was almost four. Dad would be home at six. We'd probably leave for the restaurant at seven. That gave me three hours.

I went to the telephone on the wall and dialed Trudy's number. She answered on the second ring.

44

"It's Charlie, Trudy. What are you doing?"

"Davina and I were just about to start reading our horror books. We decided not to wait until tonight. Mom fixed us some—"

"Don't!" I almost screamed into the phone. "Don't do it."

"Charlie? What's wrong with you? Why shouldn't we read them?"

"Listen, I can't explain now, but I have to talk to you both. Can you come over here?"

"Well, yeah, I guess so, but why?"

"I just said I can't explain now, but under no circumstances read those books!"

"Charlie, have you lost your mind?"

"I may have, but at least I'm still alive."

"What are you talking about?"

"I'll tell you when you get here. See you in a minute!"

Fifteen minutes later, Trudy and Davina rang the front door bell. I answered it.

"Follow me," I said.

They both gave me puzzled looks but followed anyway.

When we were downstairs in our basement, I said, "Sit down. I have something to tell you."

"Why are you acting so weird?" Trudy demanded.

"You'll see in a minute."

45

They both sat together on the sofa. I could tell they were a little scared.

"Okay, we're sitting," Davina said. "Now what's going on?"

"The book I was reading in the library today is called *Sleepover!* It's about a kid who spends the night at a friend's house and learns that his whole family sleeps in coffins. In fact, all the characters in the book do!"

"Oh, that sounds good and creepy," Davina said. "I want to read it next."

"Maybe not," I said.

Trudy looked at me. "Why?"

"I was actually *living* the story. I was right there in that kid's house, and he was trying to get me to sleep in a coffin, too." I looked at Trudy. "That's where I was when you didn't see me in the library."

"Oh, come on, Charlie, give us a break."

"It's true, and I can prove it."

Davina and Trudy looked really puzzled now. "How?" they asked.

"Look around. Do you see Dustin here?"

They looked around. "No."

"That's because he's inside *his* book."

"*Inside* his book?"

"Yes. I think these books that Ms. Gunkel put

46

in our libary pull readers into them. The readers become characters."

"This is nuts," Davina said.

"It may be, but it's true. At least I think it's true. Dustin isn't anywhere that I can find him."

"Really, Charlie! That still doesn't mean he's inside a book," Davina said. "You've been watching too much televison."

"You just have to trust me. I'm telling you what happened. I'm not making this up. I was really there."

"Couldn't you just have been daydreaming?" Davina said. "Maybe you even fell asleep."

I shook my head. "I thought about that, but it was too real. Ms. Gunkel was in the dream, too. In fact, I even talked to her."

Trudy and Davina just continued to stare at me.

"I know she's behind all of this some way. I just know she is."

"Well, what are we going to do, then?" Trudy finally said.

"I've been thinking. There has to be a reason why my book was still on the table, where you knocked it off, but Dustin's wasn't. I'm not exactly sure, but I think it may be because he was holding his book in his hand when he was reading, and I wasn't."

47

"What do you mean?" Trudy asked.

"Have you ever noticed how people read books in the library? I lay mine on the table. The only time I touch the pages is when I'm turning them."

"That's the way I do, too," Trudy said.

"I hold mine in my hand," Davina said.

"So does Dustin. So do a lot of people."

"You think that's important?" Trudy asked.

"Yes. I think if you're holding the book when you read it, then it disappears with you. If you're not holding it, then you disappear into the book, but the book stays where it was."

"This is so creepy," Davina said.

"Well even if what you say is true, Charlie, what can we do about it?" Trudy said. "How can we get Dustin back?"

"We have to go back to the library and read the book he's in," I said. "We have to read *School Trip*."

"How can we do that if he has the book?" Davina asked.

"Ms. Gunkel put duplicate copies of some of the books on the shelves. I saw them. We have to see if there's another copy of Dustin's book."

"Why do we have to read it at the library?" Trudy asked. "Why can't we just get a copy of the book and bring it back here?"

"I think you come back where you disappeared from," I replied. "That's what happened to me."

Trudy looked at her watch. "It's four-thirty. Everyone except the janitor has probably gone home by now."

"Well, Mr. Jones is usually pretty nice to us kids," I said. "I'm sure he'll let us into the library if we just tell him we need to look up something in an encyclopedia."

Trudy nodded. "Yeah. That's always a good excuse."

"But what do we do once we get a copy of Dustin's book?" Davina said. "Do we all three read it?"

"I've thought about that, too," I said. "I think Trudy and I should read it together but while it's lying on a table. That way when we disappear into the book it'll still be there."

"Don't I get to help, too?" Davina asked.

I could tell she was disappointed about not being included in Dustin's rescue operation. "You need to stay in the library so you can close the book."

"Well, how will I know when to close it?" Davina asked.

"I'll have to think about that. It needs to be long enough to rescue Dustin but not so long that we'll end up . . ."

49

"*What?*" they cried.

"I'm not sure." I looked at my watch. "We need to hurry, though. We only have a little over two hours before I'm supposed to go out to dinner with my parents. Let's get to the library, find the book, and rescue Dustin!"

We left my house and walked as fast as we could.

When we were almost to the school, I said, "What if Ms. Gunkel is still in the library? If we ask her for a copy of *School Trip,* she'll know what we're up to and won't let us have it."

"If her van's not in the parking lot, then I think we're okay," Trudy said.

Since the teacher's parking lot was on the side of the school we came to first, we knew right away that Ms. Gunkel wasn't there. We hurried as fast as we could to the back door, which was the one closest to the library.

It was locked.

I knocked several times, but nothing happened. "Are you sure Mr. Jones is still here?"

"No, I'm not," Trudy said, "but he's been here before when I've been at school late."

Davina stepped up to the door and started pounding.

That worked.

50

Mr. Jones finally opened the door, but he had a big frown on his face. "What do you kids want?"

"Oh, Mr. Jones, wouldn't you know we'd forget to do something," Trudy said. "We feel so silly."

Mr. Jones just looked at her, but the frown had disappeared. "What'd you forget to do?"

"Well, we all three have reports for English due tomorrow morning, and we have to look up something in the encyclopedia."

Mr. Jones thought for a minute. "Well, I don't know if I really should let you in or not. No one else is here."

"It's all right," Trudy said, slipping past him.

Davina and I followed.

"Well, hurry up and get it done, then," Mr. Jones called to us, as we headed down the hallway, "because I'm about to lock everything up and go home."

When we got to the library, we headed straight for the shelf containing all the new horror books.

"Who's the author?" Trudy asked.

"I don't remember," I said, "but I think it has a red and black cover."

It took us several minutes, but we finally found it.

"There's just one copy," Davina said.

"That's all we'll need," I said. "Come on."

We went to a reading table on the far side of

the library, so Mr. Jones wouldn't see us if he happened to come in.

"Let's hurry," I said breathlessly. "Davina, you sit over there in that chair. I don't want you near the book because I don't know how strong these powers are."

Davina did as I asked.

I put two chairs together next to a table, and Trudy and I sat down.

"What do we do?" Trudy asked.

I shrugged. "Why don't we just open the first page and start reading out loud together?"

Trudy took a deep breath. "Okay."

I could tell she was as scared as I was. I looked over at Davina. "Ready?"

She nodded.

I turned back to Trudy. "Ready?"

She nodded.

I took a deep breath myself and opened *School Trip* to the first page.

Trudy and I started reading.

Suddenly, it was night and we were inside a school bus. Then we passed under a streetlight and I saw that it was full of skeletons.

5

The skeletons still had on the clothes they were buried in, so you could tell the boys from the girls.

I was sitting next to a skeleton boy. Trudy was sitting in front of me next to a skeleton girl.

I looked around to make sure Davina wasn't anywhere on the bus. She wasn't. I just hoped she was still in the library, waiting to close the book when we had found Dustin.

"Where are we going?" I asked the skeleton boy.

"We're going on a school trip," he replied.

"I know, but *where* are we going?"

He turned and looked at me just as we passed under another streetlight. His teeth were all black. "To the cemetery. Where else?"

I gulped. "That's a funny place for a school trip."

53

"It's where we always go." The skeleton boy stuck out his hand. "My name was John when I was alive. What's yours?"

I shook hands with him. His bony fingers felt cold. "My name's Charlie." My voice wouldn't stay steady.

The skeleton girl sitting next to Trudy turned around and said, "Readers always say that."

"Say *what*?" I asked.

"That a cemetery is a funny place for a school trip. You get used to it after a while. Actually, it's kind of fun, thinking about who the new readers will be."

"Readers? You mean *riders*?"

"No. Readers."

Trudy shuddered.

I touched her and she jumped. "Are you all right?"

Trudy turned around slowly. There was a look of absolute terror on her face. "I think this was a mistake," she whispered. "We'll never get back home."

"Oh, yes, we will," I whispered back. "Davina will make sure we do."

"What if she doesn't close the book in time, Charlie? What then?" She turned back around before I could answer.

"I used to be a reader," the skeleton girl contin-

54

ued. She waved her skeleton hand around the bus. "Most of us did."

"What happened?" I asked.

"We finished the book before we could get back home. Now we're characters."

"You mean if you can't find a way to get back before the book's over, you become part of it forever?"

She nodded.

I had begun to break out in a cold sweat. "Well, we have to go back."

"Why should you go back if we can't?" John said to me.

I was sure nothing I could say would make any sense to him, so I changed the subject. "Have you seen another reader, a boy named Dustin? He's my age, a little chubby. He has a crew."

John shook his head.

The skeleton girl sitting next to Trudy said, "I saw him. He got on another bus because he started reading before you did. He's already at the cemetery."

My heart was about to burst through my shirt. "Do you think he's finished the book yet?"

"That depends. Is he a fast reader?"

"No."

"Then he probably hasn't."

"Maybe there's still time," Trudy whispered.

The skeleton girl sitting next to her said, "I hope not. I wish you were dead. I think we could be best friends."

That made *me* shudder. Suddenly, I thought of something. I turned to John. "Can you tell me how this book ends?"

"Well, at the cemetery . . ."

"Stop it!" the skeleton girl hissed. She looked at me. "Why should he tell you? Why can't you be surprised like the rest of us?"

"I always look at the last chapter first," I said. "I don't like surprise endings."

"Too bad!" the skeleton girl said. She turned back to Trudy. "My name was Janice when I was alive. Did you bring a lunch? If you didn't, you can share mine."

"I'm not hungry." Trudy still refused to look at the skeleton girl.

"You will be."

"No I won't!"

Just then, the bus made a sharp turn. I looked out the window. There were no more streetlights, but the moon was bright, and I could see the iron gates of a cemetery.

"We're here," Janice said. "Fairview Cemetery."

"This place is so boring," John said. "I wish we could go someplace else."

56

"This is where we go in the book," Janice said. "It can never be changed."

The bus pulled up to the front gate and stopped.

"Charlie, what's going to happen now?" Trudy asked. She had reached around and grabbed my hand.

"Everyone listen up!" The skeleton bus driver was now standing in the aisle at the front of the bus. She had turned on the overhead lights. "We're a little early, so not everyone has come out of his grave yet, but just wait patiently and they'll all be out in a little bit. Remember to be on your best behavior, too."

Yeah, right, I thought.

Everyone in the bus was now standing up. I looked around to see if there were any more readers like us. There weren't. Trudy and I were the only ones on the bus who weren't skeletons.

We held hands as we walked slowly down the aisle. I was feeling cold and clammy, like I was already dead myself.

When we finally got to the front of the bus, the driver held out her skeleton hand. "You readers will be expected to participate in all the fun and games," she said.

I swallowed hard. "What do you mean?"

The skeleton bus driver grinned, showing her

57

black teeth. "Sorry. I can't give away the ending of the book. You'll just have to keep reading."

I felt Trudy squeeze my hand even tighter.

"Just remember that Davina is in the school library, ready to close the book," I whispered.

"Don't let anybody know that or they might decide to make us read faster so we can get to the ending sooner."

I hadn't thought about that. I wasn't sure how they could make us read faster, but I agreed with Trudy. "Okay," I said.

Trudy and I left the bus. The moon was full and bright and made it relatively easy to see where we were headed.

"Don't let go of my hand, Charlie," Trudy whispered, as both our feet hit the ground at the same time. "I think these people want to make sure we never go home again."

We followed the skeleton students through the gates of the cemetery.

John must have noticed me looking around because he said, "Big, isn't it?"

"Yeah. A person could get lost here."

"It happens sometimes, especially to readers."

"Be a pal, John," I whispered to him. "Tell me what this book's about."

He looked at me and grinned. "You'll find out soon enough." Then he waved good-bye.

"Come on. Let's see if we can find Dustin," I whispered to Trudy. "Maybe the three of us can hide somewhere in the cemetery until Davina closes the book."

Trudy held back. "Oh, Charlie, I just thought of something!"

"What?"

"Dustin's not reading the same copy of the book that we are, so how can he come back with us?"

I felt a cold chill go through me. Trudy was right. I couldn't believe I'd been dumb enough to get us into this without working everything out. "Don't worry. I'll think of something." At least, I hoped I would.

"Where do you think he is, Charlie?"

"Your guess is as good as mine. Come on."

We started walking down an empty path, away from the skeleton students.

I was just sure that any minute John or Janice or the bus driver would call us back, but no one said anything. They were too busy looking for their skeleton friends, I decided.

"I wonder what kinds of games they play," I said.

"I don't want to find out," Trudy said.

"Help me!"

We stopped.

I looked at Trudy. "That sounds like Dustin!"

"Oh, Charlie. We're too late."

"Help me, please, somebody! Help me!"

"It's coming from somewhere over there," I whispered to her. "Come on!"

We began running between rows of tombstones. These were the big kind that you see in old cemeteries. It was like a miniature town, with little buildings and statues everywhere, except these buildings were tombs and the statues were all religious figures. There were a lot of angels with huge wings, and they all seemed ready to swoop down on us any minute.

"Dustin? Where are you?" I shouted.

"Help! Help!"

"Dustin!"

"Charlie? Is that you? Help me. Please, hel . . ."

Then there was nothing.

"We've got to find him, Trudy! Come on!"

We ran between several more rows of tombstones until we finally came to a crowd of skeleton kids standing around an open grave. They were all holding shovels. I pushed my way into them.

"Dustin!"

Dustin was lying on his back at the bottom of a six-foot grave. He was partially covered up with dirt. In one hand he was holding the book he had been reading. It was still open!

"What's going on here?" I demanded. "What are you doing to Dustin?"

"We're playing games. Want to join us?"

"No!" Trudy said.

"This isn't a very funny game," I said.

"It's what we like to do on school trips," one of the skeleton kids said.

Dustin was now struggling to get up. I jumped down into the grave and started helping him.

"No fair!" another one of the skeleton kids shouted. "You readers think you can change the story. Well, you can't!"

They started shoveling more dirt into the grave, but I kept trying to pull Dustin up. It didn't take long for the dirt to get in my eyes, though, and I could hardly see anything.

The skeleton kids continued to shovel dirt into the grave.

Above, I could hear Trudy screaming at them to stop.

Finally, I was able to pull Dustin up. We covered our heads and began trying to claw our way out of the grave, but the dirt kept hitting us.

"Lie down! Lie down!" the skeleton kids were shouting. "Lie down!"

"Here, let me make a hand ladder for you," I whispered to Dustin, "and then you can . . ." Suddenly it hit me. I knew now how to get Dustin

61

back. "Close the book!" I shouted. "Close the book!"

Dustin looked at me. "What?"

"Just do it!" I screamed. "Close the book!"

Dustin closed the book and disappeared.

"No fair! No fair!" the skeleton kids shouted when they realized Dustin was gone. They began to shovel faster and soon the grave dirt was up to my ankles.

"Give me your hand, Charlie!" Trudy cried. She began pulling me out.

Finally, with her help, I made it and lay panting on the ground for several minutes.

The skeleton kids had now stopped shoveling. It hadn't even occurred to me before that the skeleton kids could have pushed me back into the grave, but they didn't. I guessed that wasn't part of the story.

"You'll be sorry," one of them said. "We don't like readers who cheat."

They took their shovels and started walking slowly away from the grave site. I knew we'd see them again if Davina didn't hurry up and close the book we were reading.

"Oh, that was close," Trudy whispered. She looked around. "Do you think Dustin's back in the library?"

"I hope so."

"What do we do now?"

"We've got to hide until Davina closes the book," I said. "Come on!"

Trudy and I started down one of the paths in the opposite direction from which the skeleton kids with the shovels had gone. This part of the cemetery looked much, much older. There were trees with Spanish moss hanging almost to the ground.

"This is really scary," Trudy said.

"What'd you expect? It's a cemetery in a horror book!"

"Do you think the skeleton kids will find us back here?"

"I don't know. I just wish I knew what this book was all about. Then I'd know what not to do."

"Couldn't we hide inside one of these buildings?" Trudy said. "I'm getting cold."

"These *buildings* are where dead people are buried, Trudy. I don't want to hide in one of *those*."

"Readers? Oh, readers? Where are you?" a voice echoed in the darkness.

"Don't answer," I whispered. I looked around frantically. "I wonder if there's another way out?"

"What do you mean?" Trudy whispered back.

"I don't know why I didn't think of this before,

63

but why do we have to stay here? Why can't we just wait somewhere else until Davina closes the book?"

"That's a good idea," Trudy said. "Even if there's no back gate, we could climb over the fence and get away."

"Come on!" I whispered.

We started running down another one of the paths, away from the direction in which the voice had come.

The tombstones were almost whizzing by us now. The trees were getting thicker and the moss heavier.

Suddenly, Trudy stopped. "Oh, Charlie, I can't run anymore. I'm out of breath."

I was out of breath, too. I looked over at one of the tombstones. "I don't believe this!" I managed to heave.

"What?" Trudy said.

"Look at the dates on these graves. These people died two hundred years from now. What's happening?"

Trudy walked on down the path a few more feet. "These graves are even farther into the future, Charlie. They must keep going on and on forever." She turned to me. "There *is* no end to this. There *is* no back fence."

I thought for just a minute. "Okay. We'll just

have to take our chances at the front gate, then, but I think we can do it. If we stay off the paths and behind some of the gravestones, maybe no one will see us."

We started walking, but when we turned a corner, the skeleton kids with the shovels were waiting for us.

"You went too far," one of them said.

"What do you mean?" I asked, trying to keep my voice steady.

"Your graves are back this way. You passed them."

"*Our* graves?" Trudy said.

"Yes. You both died in the same year. You were buried next to each other."

"No!" I screamed.

The skeleton kids started laughing.

"We have to put you in your graves," another one said.

"No way!" Trudy cried. "Come on!" She grabbed my hand and started down another path at right angles to the skeleton kids. "We might be able to make it if we don't stop."

But the skeleton kids were right behind us.

"You'll never get away!" they screamed.

I looked over my shoulder. They were gaining on us.

65

"Hurry! Hurry!" I said, more to myself than to Trudy.

We kept running and turning. I was hoping that Trudy had a sense of which direction we were going because I was totally lost.

"You can't get away!" the skeleton kids kept screaming.

I looked over my shoulder and they were even closer now. They were right, I was sure. They'd bury us in our graves before Davina closed the book.

Trudy screamed as a skeleton hand grabbed her shoulder.

Then all of a sudden we were lying on the floor of the library, our tongues hanging out, panting.

When I was finally able to catch my breath, I looked up at Davina and said, "What took you so long?"

"Mr. Jones came in here once looking for us!"

"You're kidding!" I said.

"No! He almost discovered Dustin, too. I told him you two had gone to your classroom to get some pencils. I don't know if he believed me or not. He stayed here for a few minutes, talking about my last school and what my parents did and stuff like that. I couldn't close the book while he was here."

Oh, great, I thought. Mr. Jones almost caused us to be buried alive. I looked around. "Where *is* Dustin?"

"Over here." Dustin stood up slowly from the other side of the table. He was covered with mud. "My mother's going to kill me!"

"Maybe not," I said. "Let's get out of here and we'll regroup in our basement."

We made it out of the building without being

seen by Mr. Jones. When we got back to my house, we used the back stairs to get to our basement, so my parents wouldn't see us, either.

"There's a shower in the bathroom down here, Dustin. Go take one!" I said. "I'll go upstairs to my room and do the same and bring down some of my clothes for you." I turned to Trudy. "What about you? I guess you could wear something of Mom's."

Trudy shook her head. "Thanks. I'm all right. You two were the ones who were almost buried alive."

I headed up the stairs. Mom and Dad were sitting in the kitchen. I told them I'd be ready to go to the restaurant in a few minutes, then I left before they could ask any questions.

I took a quick shower and changed.

Then I got Dustin a shirt and some of my jeans and hurried back down to the basement.

Trudy had been telling Davina everything that had happened to us.

"I can't believe I almost didn't close that book in time!"

"Well, you did, and we're here," I said, "and I'm going to confront Ms. Gunkel tomorrow. I know she's behind all of this."

We all agreed to meet at school the next morning at eight o'clock and go straight to the library.

We probably should start with Mr. Scoville, I knew, but even if he believed us, which he probably wouldn't, he'd just say, "I told you so," and we'd never again be able to read horror books in school.

It took me forever to go to sleep that night. I didn't know if it was from the Mexican food or because of what had happened in the book.

When I finally did fall asleep I was back in the cemetery, being chased by the skeleton kids with shovels.

I woke up around three o'clock, covered with sweat, and decided to go downstairs to watch television.

I must have fallen asleep again because Mom woke me up at seven, when she got up.

"What are you doing in here, Charlie?"

"I didn't want to sleep in my room," I said.

She just shook her head. She knew something strange had been going on during the last few hours, but I was just glad she had decided not to ask any questions.

I fixed my own breakfast, then I went back upstairs, showered, and got ready for school.

At a quarter to eight, Dad said he'd take me if I wanted him to because it looked like it was going to rain.

"Okay," I said. I was beginning to get sleepy again, and I didn't want to walk.

He dropped me off in front of the school. I saw Trudy, Davina, and Dustin waiting for me at the front door.

I hurried up to them. "Ready?" I said. I was nervous about confronting Ms. Gunkel, but I wanted to get it over with.

"There are five other kids missing, Charlie," Trudy said. "The police just left."

I was stunned. I didn't know why I hadn't thought about that before. Other kids had been reading the horror books, too. It was logical for some of them to disappear into them. Actually, I was surprised that only five had disappeared. "Who are they?"

Trudy had written down their names. "Anne McBain, Ralph Brett, Nancy Cannell, Ed Keating, and Bill Gorman."

"What were they reading?" I asked.

They all shrugged.

"The only way we can find that out is to check the computer in the library," Dustin said, "and I'm sure Ms. Gunkel won't let us do that."

"Does anyone suspect that it was because of the horror books?" I asked.

"I don't think so," Davina replied. "Everyone

just thinks they were kidnapped, but they're trying to figure out how it's all connected."

"They'll never figure it out," I said. "It's too crazy."

More and more kids were beginning to arrive for school, so we went inside and headed for our classrooms. We decided to keep our ears open and find out what we could from the other kids and from the teachers and then talk again at recess.

Dustin and I had been in the same classes since the second grade. I really didn't want Mrs. Segrigg this year, but Dustin's mother insisted that he have her, so what else could I do but go along? It really hadn't been too bad.

Nobody wanted to do anything in class. Not even Mrs. Segrigg, which was very unusual.

"I am so upset about the five students who disappeared, I didn't sleep at all last night," Mrs. Segrigg said. "If you know anything, *anything* at all, please just tell me, and I'll make sure that the proper authorities are notified. I won't even tell them who told me."

She was pleading so hard I almost raised my hand and told her they had disappeared into the horror books they were reading, but I knew she'd think I was just trying to be cute and probably send me to the principal's office, so I kept quiet

71

and listened to the other stories the rest of the class had.

"My dad was in a convenience store late last night," Nathan Juniper said, "and he saw this gray van with all five of them in it driving by."

Mrs. Segrigg's eyes were beginning to bulge out of her head. "Really?"

Nathan nodded. "There was this old guy with a gray beard driving it, too, and he looked really mean."

Mrs. Segrigg was writing furiously on a piece of paper. "Has your father reported this to the police?"

"My mom did," Nathan replied.

"My mom thinks that aliens abducted them," Carly Besame said. "She's reading this book about how aliens from other planets come into your house at night and take you back to their spaceships."

"I bet that's where they are," George Debson said. "They always were kind of spacy."

Several of the kids laughed.

Mrs. Segrigg tapped a ruler on her desk. "This is not a humorous situation, George, and I'll thank you to be a little more serious about it. What if you had been kidnapped? I don't think your parents would want other kids laughing about it."

George slunk down in his seat and didn't say anything else.

Dustin and I looked at each other and rolled our eyes. Then I suddenly had an idea. I raised my hand.

"Yes, Charlie?"

"I really don't feel like studying, Mrs. Segrigg. I am so upset about what has happened to my friends."

Mrs. Segrigg nodded in sympathy.

"I was wondering if we could just go to the library and read. I think that might help get our minds off this."

"I agree, Charlie, but we'll have to stay in here and read today. Ms. Gunkel called in sick, and Mr. Scoville has asked us not to use the library today unless it is absolutely necessary. It seems Ms. Gunkel is very particular about who uses her computer to check books in and out."

"You mean Ms. Gunkel's not at school?"

"No." Mrs. Segrigg pointed at the metal book rack next to the door. "If you don't have something at your desk, you should be able to find something over there."

That wasn't what I had in mind. What I wanted to do was get inside the library and get into the computer so I could find out what the

73

five missing kids had been reading. With Ms. Gunkel gone, it'd be a cinch.

I raised my hand again.

"What is it, Charlie?" Mrs. Segrigg said. She sounded exasperated.

"Well, I've read all of the books in the book rack, and I was thinking that if we went to the library you could make a list of the books we got and give it to Ms. Gunkel when she came back to school and then she could put it all into the computer herself."

Mrs. Segrigg sighed.

I was beginning to try her patience, I knew, but I was getting desperate. Those five kids had started reading the books yesterday during library period and if we didn't do something soon it would be too late. They would become characters forever.

"Please try to find something, Charlie. I'm too upset about what has happened to do anything this morning. If you're not interested in reading, then I don't mind if you just talk, if you'll do it quietly."

That appealed to everyone, so I knew I'd make them mad at me if I kept it up, but I had to get to the library and find out what books those missing kids were reading.

I thought for a couple of minutes, then I said

74

to Dustin, "I've got an idea. You go over and stand near the book rack."

Dustin did as I asked.

I went up to Mrs. Segrigg's desk, where she was listening intently to another version of what had happened to the five students. This time Martie Nickles was telling her that she thought it was a terrorist group, similar to the one she'd seen on television last night.

"Excuse me, Mrs. Segrigg. Dustin and I need to go see Mr. Scoville about a matter."

Without looking at me, she said, "Well, all right, but hurry back. You know he doesn't like a lot of students in the halls during classes."

"Yes, ma'am," I said and headed toward the door.

No one paid any attention to us when we left.

"What are we going to do?" Dustin whispered to me as we started down the hall.

"We're going to Mrs. Zenzer's class and tell her we've been sent from the office to get Trudy and Davina, and then we're going to the library."

Everyone in Mrs. Zenzer's class was talking about the five missing students, too, and trying to figure out what had happened to them.

It was easy to get Trudy and Davina out of class.

"What if Mr. Scoville sees us?" Trudy said.

75

"I'm quite sure Mr. Scoville has his hands full," I said. "After all, five students from his school have disappeared. He'll probably be in his office all morning, on the telephone or talking to the police or upset parents."

We made it to the library without being seen, but we decided not to turn on any of the lights in case Mr. Scoville just happened to walk by.

"What if Ms. Gunkel shows up?" Davina said. "I don't believe she's really sick."

"I don't, either, but we can't worry about that now," Trudy said. "We've got to get into the computer." She was already heading for the terminal on Ms. Gunkel's desk.

She turned it on and the menu appeared. There were only three items. She entered BOOKS PROCESSED. That got her into the program which listed the books checked out by all of the students and teachers at school.

She began entering the names of the missing students. Beside each name there appeared the title of the book that had been checked out:

ANNE MCBAIN: THE ZOMBIE WHO LIVES UNDER OUR HOUSE

RALPH BRETT: THE VAMPIRE FOOTBALL TEAM

NANCY CANNELL: THE ZOMBIE WHO LIVES UNDER OUR HOUSE

We all looked at the list.

"We're in luck," Davina said. "There are only three books we have to get into."

"Which one do we read first?" Dustin asked.

"We have to consider two things," I said. "We have to think about who the fast readers are, and we have to think about what kinds of problems we'd have with each book."

"What do you mean, *problems*?" Trudy asked.

"We were almost buried alive in *School Trip*. We want to make sure the first book we read will be the easiest to get out of and then work our way up to the hardest one."

"I don't understand," Davina said.

"If we start with the book that'll give us the most trouble, then we might not make it back to get into the others."

"Oh. Now, I see what you mean," Dustin said. He looked at the titles again. "Which one looks the scariest?"

Davina shivered. "*The Vampire Football Team*. I hate vampires."

"Me, too," I said. "I say we do the werewolves first, the zombies second, and the vampires last."

"Who's going?" Dustin asked.

77

"I sort of feel responsible, so I'll go on all of them," I said, "but the rest of you only have to go on one."

"Why should you go on all of them?" Davina asked.

I had anticipated this question. "Because I've read more horror books than anyone else at Edison Elementary School, that's why. I consider myself an expert, because I can usually figure out the plot twists before they happen."

For a minute, I didn't think Davina was going to accept my explanation, but she didn't say anything, mainly because Trudy and Dustin agreed with me.

"I think it might be a good idea for there to be *two* of you ready to close the book, though, just in case something happens like happened last night when Mr. Jones stayed to talk to Davina."

"Are we going to do it here in the library?" Trudy asked.

"We have to. This is where they were reading when they were pulled into the story. This is where they'll come back when I tell them to close their books."

"Then let's get started," Davina said. She got the duplicate copies of the three books off the shelf. "I'll go with Charlie on *Werewolves at Summer Camp*."

We all went to the far side of the library, where we'd be hidden by the shelves from anyone looking in through the doors, but where we'd also have some light from the windows to read by.

Davina and I sat down together. We lay the book on the floor in front of us. Since Bill had already been reading for several hours, we decided to start a third of the way into it.

All of a sudden, we were standing in front of a wood cabin in the middle of a thick forest and we were surrounded by howling wolves.

7

"Let's check out this cabin first," I whispered to Davina.

"Good idea. Anything to get away from those horrible howling noises."

I opened the door and stuck my head inside. "Anybody in here?"

"Yes," a voice said. It sent chills through me.

I took a deep breath and stepped inside. Davina was right behind me.

A match flickered and then a lamp was lit.

A boy about my age was lying on a bed in the corner of the room. "This isn't the beginning. You're not supposed to be here yet."

"Where are we?" I asked.

"You're in the middle of chapter four," the boy replied. "Where did you think you were?"

"I mean, where is this *place?*"

"It's Camp Long Lake. It's the camp the werewolves attack in the book." The boy sat up. "I'm not supposed to be telling you all this, though. Why didn't you start at the beginning like you were supposed to?"

I swallowed hard. "Look, we're trying to find a friend of ours by the name of Bill Gorman and we don't have a lot of time."

"He's here. He got to camp yesterday. He's probably already been bitten by the werewolves, though." He looked at us for several minutes. "We've never had readers try to save other readers before. I wish someone had tried to save me. You're probably too late."

Davina gasped. "Are you sure?"

The boy shook his head. "I'm not sure of anything. You just never know how it's going to happen to readers. It's up to them to decide. This is one of those books where you choose your own ending."

I looked around. "Are you the only one in this cabin?"

The boy nodded. "This is where the really exciting part of the book starts. I'm here in my cabin, sick, because I've just been bitten by one of the werewolves, so when the readers get back from a party I try to bite them, but they get away and hide in another one of the cabins."

"Is that where Bill is now?"

The boy shrugged.

Then a strange thing started to happen. Long brown hair began appearing on his face and hands. When he opened his mouth his teeth looked pointed and sharp.

I grabbed Davina's hand and started backing out of the room. "Don't take your eyes off him," I whispered.

"Oh, Charlie, what if he tries to attack us?"

I continued to stare at the boy. "Don't think about it. Just keep backing up."

"The wolves are all round us waiting to bite everyone," the boy growled. "You'll never get away."

Then he suddenly fell to the floor on all fours, growling at us even more and showing us his fangs.

We had reached the door now.

Davina pushed it open. We turned around and ran back out into the night.

I stumbled a couple of times but stayed on my feet. Finally, we had to stop after we had both been slapped in the face by the branches of low-hanging trees.

"Is he coming after us?" Davina asked.

"I don't think so."

"Oh, Charlie, what are we going to do? We have

to find Bill, but I don't want to go inside any more of these cabins."

"I know what you mean, but we may have to. That boy said the readers all went to the other cabins."

"He's no longer a boy, Charlie, he's a *werewolf!*"

All around us the wolves continued to howl. They seemed to be getting closer and closer.

"Have you heard of this book before?" I asked Davina.

She shook her head.

"I was trying to remember if I had, from what that boy, uh, *werewolf* said. I think it's about this isolated summer camp where several kids get bitten by wolves right after they arrive and turn into werewolves. The wolves have surrounded the camp, so there's no way for the other campers to escape."

"Maybe there's no escape for us, either, Charlie."

"If Trudy closes the book in time, we'll be able to escape before anything happens to us, but we just have to keep looking for Bill. I don't want anything to happen to him, either."

The moon was very bright, which I had decided was what you always found in most horror books. I was glad, since all the stories seemed to take place at night, too.

"I know you don't want to, Davina, but I think we need to check out some of the other cabins."

Then we heard a blood-curdling cry.

"It's coming from over there!" Davina said.

Through the thick pines I thought I could see another cabin. "Come on," I whispered. "Maybe that's Bill."

The screams kept getting louder and louder.

We had reached the front of the cabin. It looked just like the first cabin we had been in.

I ran up the steps, but Davina grabbed my arm. "What if they're just waiting to attack us, Charlie?"

"We have to take that chance. We can't let Bill get bitten and turn into a werewolf."

I pulled open the screen door.

A werewolf had a boy by the arm.

"Let him go!" I cried.

The werewolf turned its head but kept the boy's arm in its mouth. I couldn't tell who the boy was.

I grabbed a baseball bat that was leaning up against the wall and swung it in the werewolf's direction.

The werewolf suddenly turned loose of the boy's arm and stood up on its two legs. "It's too late," it said in a growling voice. "We now have another reader who'll be staying at Camp Long Lake forever."

The boy's head flopped over in my direction. I'd never seen him before. I felt sorry for him, but I was glad it wasn't Bill.

I looked around the room and saw only the werewolf and the boy. It was strange. Where was everyone else?

"Let's get out of here," I whispered to Davina.

"That's a good idea," she whispered back.

Outside, I told her what I had been thinking. "Both of those cabins had just three people in them altogether. I wonder where everyone is."

"Maybe they're all hiding in one place, but where? That first boy only mentioned cabins."

"Up in the trees? Out on a lake?"

"I hadn't thought about that." I looked up. I couldn't see anyone in the trees above us. "Let's see if we can find the lake. There's always one in horror books."

"Which direction do we go?"

I shrugged. "I say we just stay on these paths. I'm sure they'll lead either to another cabin or a lake."

We started down another one of the paths. From time to time we glanced up into the trees, just in case the rest of the campers had taken refuge in them.

85

We had only gone a few yards when our way was blocked by two huge wolves.

Their mouths were open and moonlight glinted off their sharp teeth. Their eyes seems to glow red.

"Oh, Charlie, what are we going to do now?"

I didn't know why Davina kept asking me that. I had no idea. "Maybe we could climb one of these trees."

"I could never make it up high enough before the wolves reached us."

"Well, we have to do something fast," I whispered. "Look!"

The wolves had starting coming toward us. They were growling low and ominously.

We started backing up.

Within a few feet, we had reached a crosspath.

"Down this way," I said. I grabbed Davina's hand and started running. I had no idea where we were going.

The branches were slapping us in the face.

Behind us I could almost feel the wolves' breath.

Then I saw another cabin.

"We've got to make it!" I cried. "We've got to make it."

I looked over my shoulder. The wolves were

getting closer. Their red eyes seemed to have flames shooting from them.

Finally, we were at the steps to the cabin, but I tripped and fell.

"Aaaghh!" Pain shot through my leg.

"Charlie!" Davina screamed.

"Save yourself, Davina!"

The wolves were almost upon us.

Davina grabbed my arm and began dragging me up the steps. "Help, somebody! Help!" she cried. "Oh, Charlie, this can't be happening."

Now Davina was pulling me across the porch of the cabin. The wolves had reached the clearing in front.

Davina opened the screen door and pulled me inside.

She shut the door just as one of the wolves lunged at it. This flimsy screen door was now the only thing between us and them.

Then the second wolf hit the door, pushing the screen almost out of the wooden frame.

"Oh, Charlie, it'll get in. It'll kill us!"

Davina was looking frantically around the room. The wolves continued to lunge at the screen door.

"Can you hold the door?" she cried. "I'll push this chest over in front of it."

"I think I can," I said. I reached up and

grabbed the handle and hung on to it with all my might.

Davina ran over to the far side of the room and began pushing the chest over toward the door.

It seemed like forever, and I didn't think I could hold out much longer, but she finally got the chest positioned in front of the door so the wolves couldn't push the screen in.

Still, for several minutes, they butted their heads against it. Then all was quiet and Davina and I lay on the floor trying to catch our breath.

"Where do you think they went?" she asked after we hadn't heard the wolves for several minutes.

"I'm sure they're still out there."

She crawled over to a window and peeked out. "You're right. They're both lying on the bottom steps. Oh, Charlie, they'll never let us out."

"They have to. We can't just stay here. If we don't find Bill soon, Trudy and Dustin will close the book, and we'll never get him back!"

Suddenly, I thought of something. "Come with me," I whispered.

Davina and I began crawling on our stomachs toward the rear of the cabin.

Each cabin was one large room, but there were screened windows all around. The back of the cabin was up against the trees. The branches actually touched the screens.

"If we can push this screen off, then we can get out," I whispered.

"Won't the wolves hear us?" Davina asked.

I shrugged. "I don't know. We'll just have to take that chance. Anyway, even if they come around to this side, they won't be able to get in, I don't think, because the windows are too high."

I got in a crouch and started pushing against the metal screen, but it wouldn't give.

"Why don't you push on the opposite corner?" I whispered to Davina.

She did.

Together we were finally able to get the screen loose without too much noise, but we waited for several minutes to see if the wolves would come around back.

They didn't.

I crawled back over to the front of the cabin and peeked out the front screen. The two wolves were still lying on the front porch, their red eyes glowing in the moonlight.

Then I crawled to the back of the cabin. Davina had already moved a chair so we could stand on it to get out the window.

"I'll go first," she said.

I didn't argue with her.

She stood on the chair, put a leg through the

window, pushing the metal screen out, and then balanced herself on the frame.

She swung the other leg over and then hopped to the ground.

There were no howls from the front porch, which I hoped meant the wolves were still there, lying in wait for us.

Then I did the same as Davina.

When we were both on the ground, we could hardly move because the trees were so close.

"We can't keep running through the woods checking out each cabin, Charlie. There's just not time. If we don't do something fast, the wolves will make their final assault on the camp and none of us will get back home."

The howling noises in the woods around us kept getting closer and closer.

Finally, we were able to crawl to the corner of the cabin. From there, we could see several feet down another path. For a minute, I thought my eyes were deceiving me, but there in a clearing was a circle of werewolves and in the middle was Bill Gorman. In his hand he held the book he had been reading. It was still open.

The werewolves were on all fours and had Bill surrounded. His eyes were wide with terror.

They kept getting closer and closer and closer to him.

"Tell him to close the book, Charlie!" Davina whispered.

"We have to get closer, Davina. He's too terrified to do anything. They'll attack him before he understands what I mean."

"But what else can we do?"

"Fire," I said. "Fire frightens wolves. Maybe it'll frighten werewolves, too."

"Fire?" Davina said.

I nodded and started back toward the window we'd just escaped from. "There have to be some matches around here somewhere. There are always matches at camp. You need them for campfires."

I tried to hoist myself back up into the window, but I couldn't make it.

"Here. Let me," Davina said. "Make a handhold and then lift me up."

In just a few seconds she was back inside. I could hear her rummaging around in the different duffel bags. I only hoped the wolves on the front porch couldn't hear her.

Finally, she reappeared at the window. "I found some. Now, what do we do?"

"We make a torch," I replied.

I helped Davina out and then we found a dead branch with leaves. Davina took one of the matches and lit it.

When it had a pretty good flame, we started

back toward the circle where Bill was surrounded by the werewolves.

"Bill!" I shouted.

"What? Who is it?"

"Charlie Stanton!"

Bill was trying to look past the werewolves, who were getting even closer. "Help me, Charlie! Help me!"

One of the werewolves looked my way and I thrust the torch at it.

It growled and withdrew.

That helped us get even closer.

Soon the werewolves had broken the circle and were trying to decide how to react to the fire.

They were drawing into small groups, growling at us and baring their teeth, but they all seemed to be afraid of the torch.

Davina and I were inside the circle now, next to Bill.

"What happened? How did I get here? How did you find me?"

"It's a really long story, but it'll be over in a few minutes, if you'll just do what I say," I whispered. "Close your book now!"

For just a second, Bill looked puzzled, but then he closed his book and disappeared.

"Look, Charlie!" Davina cried. She was pointing to the end of the torch. It had almost burned down to nothing.

The werewolves had seen it, too, and were slowly starting back toward us. This time, I knew, they wouldn't just circle us, they'd bite us with their sharp teeth.

I started blowing on the torch, trying to restart the flames, but nothing happened, except that the ends of the branches began to glow. They wouldn't flame up.

The werewolves kept getting closer and closer.

They had now reformed their circle, so there was no escape.

"We could try to run for a weak link," Davina whispered.

"It's no use," I whispered.

Then one of the werewolves lunged at me.

It was like a slow-motion movie, as the huge creature bared its sharp teeth and aimed for my neck.

I raised my leg to stop the attack.

I felt a sharp pain, as the werewolf's teeth cut into it, and then I was lying on the floor of the library.

"Oh, Charlie!" Trudy cried. "Your leg's all covered with blood!"

"What happened to you?" Dustin asked. He was looking at my bloody leg.

"He was bitten by a werewolf," Davina said. "It was terrible!"

Bill was sitting up, rubbing his eyes, and looking in amazement around the library. "How'd I get back here?"

I quickly explained what had happened to him and how I thought Ms. Gunkel was behind it.

"That's crazy," Bill said. "How could she be?"

"Only Ms. Gunkel knows the answer to that," Trudy said, "and we can't ask her until we've rescued the other kids."

Trudy handed me a copy of *The Zombie Who Lives Under Our House.* "I want to go with you on this one," she said. "Anne and Nancy are good friends of mine."

"I'll go with you on the next one," Dustin said. "Ralph and Ed are good friends of mine."

"We need to put a bandage on your leg before you go anywhere, Charlie," Davina said.

"We don't have time. We have to—"

Davina stopped me. "There's probably a medicine kit in the nurse's office. I'll go get it. It won't take long. There's no telling what might happen if you don't take care of that. After all, it's a *werewolf* bite."

I knew she was right, so I didn't try to stop her. I wasn't quite sure how Davina planned to get it, but I was sure she'd be able to.

While Davina was gone, I told Dustin and Trudy everything that happened to us at Camp Long Lake. Bill filled in with the details of what had happened before we got there.

Trudy shuddered. "It sounds awful."

"It was," I agreed. "If we hadn't started in chapter four, we would never have been able to bring Bill back."

"Should we start in the middle of *The Zombie Who Lives Under Our House?*" Trudy asked.

"I've been thinking about that. We probably need to start past the middle."

"That makes sense. Anne and Nancy are fast readers. That's probably where they are."

"I hope so," I said. "We don't want to start past

where they are, because then we'll be ahead of them and never find them."

"I hadn't thought of that," Trudy said.

"What would happen then?" Bill asked.

"We'd get to the end of the book and if no one had closed it we'd become characters forever."

"I met some kids in *Werewolves at Summer Camp* that had happened to," Bill said. He shuddered.

I nodded, remembering all of the readers I had met who were now characters in their books.

"Imagine being a character in a horror book forever. These awful things keep happening to you over and over as each new person reads it!"

Just then we heard someone coming into the library.

"That's probably Davina," I said.

Then the overhead lights went on.

Trudy, who could see the door from where she was behind the shelves, said, "No! It's Ms. Gunkel! I knew she wasn't sick!"

"This is awful!" I said. "What if she finds us and makes us give back the duplicate copies of these horror books?"

"We'll never be able to get the rest of the other kids back if she does that!" Bill said.

"She won't find us unless she comes over here behind these shelves," Trudy said.

"What's she doing?" I whispered to Trudy.

Trudy moved her head so she could see over the top of the books on the bottom shelf. "She's at her computer."

We held our breath.

"What's she doing now?" I asked a couple of minutes later.

"She's going over to the shelf where the horror books are."

Oh, no! I thought.

Then we heard angry muttering.

"She knows the duplicates are missing!" Trudy whispered.

Suddenly we heard the door to the library opening again.

"What are you doing in here?" Ms. Gunkel demanded. "The library's closed today!"

This had to be Davina, coming back with the medicine for my leg. It was really throbbing now and I was beginning to worry that the werewolf bite was bad and I'd become sick somehow.

"Oh, I didn't know," Davina said. "I saw the lights on. I just wanted to get a book to read."

"You can get one tomorrow. I'm not supposed to be here today. I'm sick. I just came in to check on something. Go back to class."

"It won't take but just a minute, Ms. Gunkel," Davina persisted.

I heard a chair scraping on the floor. "What do you have in your hands?" Ms. Gunkel demanded.

"Nothing," Davina said.

"Let me see!"

"If you're not going to let me check out a book, then I need to get back to class," Davina said hurriedly. We heard the door to the library close.

"What's happening now? Is she going after her?" I whispered to Trudy.

Trudy maneuvered her head so she could get a better look. "No. She's just standing there."

Ms. Gunkel stood there for what seemed like hours, then she turned out the lights and left the library. We heard a clicking sound, and we knew that she had locked the door from the outside.

"How are we going to get out?" Dustin said.

"Don't worry," I said. "You just have to push the release bar."

"Oh, yeah."

"How'll Davina get back in, though?" Trudy asked.

"I'll go get her," I said. I stood up.

"I don't think we should do anything for a few minutes until we're sure Ms. Gunkel is gone for good."

We waited for several minutes. Then we heard a soft knocking on the door.

"Who's that?" Trudy whispered.

"It has to be Davina," I said. I stood up again. "I'll go open the door."

Trudy grabbed my hand. "It could be a trick, Charlie. It may be Ms. Gunkel instead."

My throbbing leg told me I couldn't wait to find out. I had to take care of it and then get inside the next book.

I started out from behind the bookshelves. It hurt to walk. I wasn't sure I was going to make it to the door of the library, let alone through a book called *The Zombie Who Lives Under Our House*.

But I did. Davina was standing there almost in a panic. She hurried into the library and I pulled the door shut.

"Did you hear all of that?"

I nodded.

"She almost caught me again when she was leaving."

"Did you get the medicine kit?" I whispered to her. "My leg's killing me."

"Yes. I don't know what's in here, though. I just grabbed the closest one and ran."

We went back over to where Dustin, Trudy, and Bill were waiting for us. Now, I was having to drag my leg behind me.

"Charlie, I don't think you're really up to this," Trudy said. "I think someone else should go."

"I have to!" I said. "I feel responsible!"

I sat down and pulled up the leg of my jeans. The bite looked horrible. Trudy was probably right. I was already feeling light-headed. I doubted if I'd make it, but I wasn't going to tell them that.

Davina poured iodine all over it and then criss-crossed it with bandages. I had to grit my teeth because it stung so much.

When the burning stopped, I said, "We've got to go, Trudy!"

She looked at me, gave a big sigh, and then said, "All right."

We positioned the book on the floor between us and opened it about two thirds of the way.

"The rest of you look the other direction," I said. "We won't touch the book, so it'll still be here when we disappear into it. Dustin, it'll be your job to close it, but you can all decide together when you need to do it. It'll just be a guess. I just hope we're at the part where Anne and Nancy are."

The three of them turned their heads.

Trudy and I had only read two lines when we were suddenly in the garden of a huge old mansion surrounded by palm trees and a jungle. Standing at the gate, swaying back and forth, was a zombie.

It started walking toward us.

Trudy grabbed my hand and pulled me toward the front door of the mansion. "Where do you think we are?"

The pain in my leg was almost more than I could stand. "It's probably some place in the South or on some tropical island. That's usually where zombie stories take place."

Trudy opened the front door, and we were inside a huge room that had a winding staircase at the end of it.

"There are probably plenty of places to hide here," she said. "Maybe Anne and Nancy are in one of the rooms."

We ran up the stairs and hurried as fast as we could from room to room, with me limping all the way, but no one was inside of any of them.

"That's strange," I said. "In the last book, we found several characters right away."

Then we heard drums.

Trudy ran to a window and looked out. "Oh, Charlie! I think that's them."

"Where?" I asked.

She pointed.

Just beyond the garden where we had been, I could see two zombies in the moonlight. They were each carrying a girl in their arms. They

101

were heading toward a grove of trees beyond the house.

"Are you sure it's them?"

"No, but we can't take a chance. We have to find out!" She turned and ran from the room. I followed her as best I could, but the throbbing in my leg had gotten worse.

When we reached the bottom of the stairs, the garden zombie was standing at the front door.

"What's he doing?" Trudy whispered.

"He's probably there to keep us from following the other zombies."

Trudy looked around frantically. "There has to be a back entrance. Come on!" She grabbed my hand and we starting running toward the back part of the mansion. My leg felt like it was on fire, but I knew we couldn't stop.

Finally, we reached the back door.

I opened it slowly and peeked out. There was no one around. Trudy and I slipped through it, then made our way around the house to the garden.

The zombie was still standing in the front doorway but his back was to us now.

We ran through the garden in the direction we had seen the zombies carrying the girls we thought were Anne and Nancy.

All around us the drums continued.

102

"What's going on here?" Trudy asked. "Why the drums?"

"It's probably a voodoo ceremony," I said.

"Oh, no, Charlie! People who practice voodoo are supposed to be able to bring dead people back alive!" She stopped. "Do you think Anne and Nancy are already dead? Do you think those zombies are taking them somewhere to turn them into zombies, too?"

I didn't even want to think about that. "Maybe not," I said. "We'll just have to find out!"

Now we were running through sugarcane. I wasn't surprised. Characters in zombie books always run through it. The path we were following was barely wide enough for one person. The drums were getting louder, too. I knew we were headed in the right direction.

Then we came to a place where two paths crossed.

"Which way?" Trudy asked.

The sugarcane was almost twice as high as our heads. The drums continued to beat all around us. "I don't know."

My leg no longer felt like it was on fire. In fact, I couldn't feel anything, and that scared me even more.

"Are you all right?" Trudy asked. She was breathing hard.

"I'm okay," I replied, but she knew I was lying.

Then we saw a zombie. He was coming from the same direction we had. It was the zombie who had been guarding the front door of the old mansion.

I made a quick decision and kept going straight.

But we only went a few yards before I realized I had made a mistake. We had reached a dead end.

"Charlie! Look!"

I turned and looked where Trudy was pointing, back down the path. In the moonlight we could no longer see the zombie.

"He wasn't coming after us after all. He was going to the ceremony."

We turned around and started running back toward where the paths crossed.

When we reached it, we could just barely see the zombie.

"We'll follow him but not so close that he'll notice."

Actually, it was hard for me to believe that a dead person could notice anything, but I didn't want to take a chance.

We kept the zombie in sight, which wasn't all

that difficult because he wasn't walking very fast.

Suddenly, up ahead, the zombie entered a clearing in the sugarcane and disappeared.

Trudy and I got as close to the edge of the sugarcane field as I thought we could without being seen.

From where we were standing now, we could see people dancing around a huge fire. They all seemed oblivious to each other. From time to time, some of them would fall onto the ground and start screaming.

Trudy gasped.

The dancers had stopped and the two zombies we had seen earlier were now coming from a wooden shack at the edge of the clearing. They were still carrying the two girls.

"Oh, Charlie! They both have open books in their hands! It is Anne and Nancy!" Trudy whispered. "What are the zombies going to do with them?"

"I have no idea. I don't know the plot of this book."

We didn't have to wait long to find out, though. The zombies set them down, one on each side of the fire. Anne and Nancy just stood still, staring out into space.

Then the people in the circle began to dance

around them again. The chants grew louder and louder. So did the drums.

"They *are* turning them into zombies!" Trudy cried. "We have to stop the ceremony!"

I was thinking fast. All of the dancers seemed totally out of it and once again oblivious to what was going on.

"If we rush in and tell Annie and Nancy to close their books, then maybe we could be back out into the sugarcane fields before anyone realizes what we've done."

"I think that's our only chance," Trudy whispered. "We could then run back to the mansion and hide until Davina closes the book we're reading."

I was worried that Anne and Nancy were under some spell and wouldn't understand me when I told them to close their books, but we had to take the chance.

"Okay. On three!"

On three we dashed into the clearing and through the dancers in the circle. I was getting pretty good at dragging my left leg, but I was having to bite my lip because it was hurting so much.

"Close your book, Anne!" I shouted. "Close your book, Nancy!"

For just a minute, nothing happened, then they

both blinked. "Close your books!" I screamed at them. "Now!"

This time they did what I told them. As soon as their books were closed, they disappeared from the circle.

"We're out of here!" I shouted at Trudy.

Everything had happened so quickly, we were several yards down the path in the sugarcane field before the drums stopped and people started shouting at us.

They were speaking a language I had never heard before, but I didn't need anyone to tell me that they had discovered that Anne and Nancy were missing and were coming after us.

Suddenly my leg gave way and I fell to the ground.

"Charlie! Get up!" Trudy cried. "They're coming!"

"You go on," I said. "I'll wait here until Davina closes the book."

"I won't leave you," Trudy said. "Let's hide in the sugarcane."

The stalks were so close together, it was almost impossible to get into it, but we finally managed just as people started running past us.

Finally, they were all past and we let out our breath.

Then I heard a noise at the edge of the break.

I looked up and saw three zombies standing there. The biggest one parted the sugarcane and started toward us.

Trudy screamed.

Then we were lying on the floor in the library several feet away from Anne and Nancy. I tried to stand up, but I couldn't.

"You'll never be able to play football," Dustin said.

I looked up at him. "What are you talking about? I don't play football now."

He shoved a book in my face. *"The Vampire Football Team.* That's the next book we have to read. It's the one Ralph and Ed are in."

Oh, great! I had forgotten about that. I pulled up my pants leg. Where the werewolf had bitten me was all red and swollen. "I think it's infected."

"We have to call a doctor," Davina said. "You could lose your leg if we don't. I saw something like this in a movie once."

I made myself stand up. Pain shot through my leg like a thousand needles sticking in it. "I'll be all right," I lied. "Let me see the book."

Dustin handed it to me. "I'm going with you, remember?"

"No, you're not. I've decided I'm the only one going this time."

"What do you mean? You can't do this by yourself. I'm going with you!"

"Look, Dustin, this is the last book. We have to start toward the end because for Ralph and Ed it's probably almost over."

"But that's the exciting part, Charlie. There's no telling what will happen. You need me to help you."

"I've made my decision. There's no sense taking a chance on both of us becoming permanent characters." I turned to Trudy. "It'll be up to you to close the book. It's going to be close because there are only a few pages left."

"Okay," Trudy said, but I could tell she was scared.

I sat back down on the floor.

Dustin was angry and whirled around so his back would be to me, but his shoe hit my leg and I cried out in pain.

"Charlie, you can't go!" Davina said.

I took a deep breath. I knew if I didn't start soon I might be talked out of it, so I started reading the next to last chapter.

Then somebody hit me.

I was under a pile of football players, but they were all vampires.

Somewhere in the distance, a whistle blew.

One of the players bared his fangs at me. "Next time it'll be your throat," he said.

When they had finally all unpiled, one of the players from my team pulled me up.

"Fill me in on the plot," I whispered.

He looked at me. "You're a reader, aren't you?"

I nodded.

"I used to be a reader. Now I'm a character." He sighed. "You're in the middle of the final game. If we lose, the vampires get us."

"What if we win?"

"We won't win. That's the way the book ends."

Not if I can help it, I thought. "I'm looking for two friends of mine. Ralph Brett and Ed Keating. Have you seen them?"

"They've been taken out with injuries. I think they're in the locker room."

"I have to find them." I started off the field.

A whistle blew.

The player grabbed me by the arm. "You can't leave the game. The coach won't let you."

"I have an injury, too." I showed him the part of my leg that was showing below my football pants.

"You didn't get that injury in this book, though, so it doesn't count." He pulled me back into the huddle.

I was a tight end and the ball was going to be thrown to me on this play. I didn't think I could run at all with my leg hurting the way it was, but I knew I had to try.

The quarterback barked the signals.

The vampire lined up in front of me was baring his fangs. "We're out for blood!" he said. Then he started laughing. "You won't have any left after this play."

"That's what you think," I said.

When the center snapped the ball, I ran around the vampire player and then headed to my right. My leg was killing me, but I had to complete this play.

I was supposed to be in position to get the ball after I completed the bottom of an *S* pattern.

I had done that.

Now, over my shoulder, I could see the ball coming toward me.

Two vampires were giving chase, but I reached up and pulled the ball in.

I was running along the sidelines on the vampire side of the field. They were all screaming and baring their fangs.

I knew all the football players were vampires, but now I could see that so were the cheerleaders and the people in the stands.

I had reached the vampires' 40-yard line. I had

clear sailing in front of me to make a touchdown if my leg would just hold up, but behind me two vampires were closing in fast. I couldn't believe how fast they were running. With my leg, I'd never make it to the goal line, I knew.

They'd get me before I made the touchdown and sink their teeth into my neck.

I tried to run faster, but it was useless. My sides were about to split.

Then all of a sudden I was on the floor in the library again.

"What happened?" I cried.

"We thought you were at the end of the book," Trudy said.

"No. It's not over yet. I was running for a touchdown."

"We didn't want you to become a character," Davina said.

"I have to go back! Ralph and Ed are injured." I took a deep breath. "I'll start three pages into the last chapter and see what happens. They're probably in the locker room by now. I think I can have them out in just a few minutes."

Trudy handed me the book. I turned to the last chapter, flipped three pages over, and started reading.

Now, I was lying together with the other players on my team on wet cement in what must be the locker room, but it looked more like a dungeon. The odor was awful. I raised my head. Ralph and Ed were on the opposite side of the room. *But they didn't have their books in their hands!*

The members of the vampire football team had us surrounded. "We won! We won!" they were chanting. "We want their blood! We want their blood!"

Slowly, I began crawling on my stomach over toward where Ralph and Ed were. I had to get them out of here and find out where their books were.

"What are you going to do to us?" our coach demanded.

"You'll see," the vampire coach replied. "Stand up."

I was getting closer to Ralph and Ed.

All of our team members started standing up. I raised up in a crouch and quickly ran over to Ralph and Ed.

"Charlie!" Ralph whispered.

"Quiet!" I whispered back.

"How'd you get here?" Ed asked.

"I'll explain later. Where are the books you were reading in the library?"

"We left them in the cemetery after the pep rally," Ralph whispered.

114

"What *cemetery?*"

Ed shrugged. "It's somewhere close to the football stadium."

"Well, we've got to go back there. Your life depends on it." I looked around. To my left were some stone steps. I had no idea where they led, but we had to escape some way. "On three, run for those steps over there. Climb them as fast as you can and don't ask questions! I'll explain everything later."

"Okay," they whispered.

The three of us got ready to run.

"One, two, three!"

We ran out of the locker room and immediately found ourselves in a dark circular staircase that reminded me of a castle.

Behind us we could hear the screams of the vampires. "Get them! Get them!"

"Where does this go?" Ralph said.

My leg was on fire. "I don't know, but at least we're going up!" Of course, I wasn't so sure that was a good idea, but we kept on running anyway.

Then the steps ended, and we were in a large room lit by torches on the wall.

"It really is a castle!" I said.

Behind us, we could hear the screams of the vampires as they made their way up the stone steps.

115

"Which way now?" Ralph asked.

On the other side of the room was a huge wooden door. "This way!"

I ran to the door and opened it.

The room was full of coffins. By the torchlight, I could see they were all open and empty.

"We can hide here until we lose the vampires," I said, "then we'll find that cemetery where you left your books."

"I'm not hiding in any coffin," Ed said.

"Me, either," Ralph said.

"It's either that or have one of those vampires take out all of your blood!"

That decided it for them.

Even with the torchlight from the open door, some of the coffins around the edge of the room were almost in darkness. Those were the ones I thought we should hide in. If the vampires looked into the room, they'd only see empty open coffins.

At the back of the room, we found three coffins together.

Ralph and Ed stood beside them, while I ran back over and closed the wooden door. Now, it was darker than midnight, so I had to feel my way back to where they were.

We had planned to leave the lids up just enough to let in some air, but when we climbed inside and lay down, they slammed shut.

I tried pushing up the lid on my coffin, but it wouldn't budge. "Ralph! Ed!" I screamed. I was hoping mine was the only one that had locked and that either Ralph or Ed could get me out.

When nothing happened after several minutes, I knew their coffin lids had locked, too.

It was already getting warm. It wouldn't be long until I had used up my entire supply of oxygen.

Then the coffin started to move.

Someone was picking it up, I was sure, and I was being carried out of the room.

Were they also picking up the coffins with Ralph and Ed in them? I wondered. What a stupid idea this had been! I wanted to scream. Why had I thought hiding in coffins would delay the vampires finding us?

The coffin tilted, and I knew I was being carried down steps. They were probably the same stone steps we had run up a few minutes ago.

I was gasping for breath because there was almost no air inside my coffin. It didn't matter now where we were going, I knew. I'd be dead before we got there.

I tried holding my breath and then, when I could hold it no longer, tried breathing just a little, but I'd always end up gasping for air, and there wasn't any air to inhale.

I began to black out. Stars were swirling all around my eyes.

What was happening? Was I dying?

I struggled to raise my hands and push against the coffin lid. I had no strength, but I refused to give up.

Then the lid opened. Cold air rushed into the coffin and froze the perspiration on my body. I began coughing and gasping for air.

My eyes must have been closed because when I opened them four vampires were looking down at me. They were dressed in football uniforms.

"Ready for another game?" one of them said, baring his fangs. They were dripping blood.

"No!" I screamed.

One of the other vampires jerked me up so fast by my collar that I was hanging in midair, my feet dangling, before I realized what had happened. "The answer is yes!" he hissed. He dropped me onto the concrete floor with a thud. I landed on my throbbing leg, and for a minute I saw stars again.

Then I noticed Ralph and Ed being pulled out of the other two coffins. They were gasping and coughing like I had been, but at least they were still alive.

The vampire football team began marching us

down through the tunnel. In a few minutes, we were back on the playing field.

"We'll kick off to you," one of the vampires said.

"There are only three of us," I protested. "There are eleven of you."

"The rest of your players have been thrown out of the game," another one of the vampires said. He laughed and bared his bloody fangs. "You'll just have to do the best you can with the players you have."

They put the football on the 30-yard line and lined up in kicking formation.

"We don't have much time because the book is almost over," I said to Ralph and Ed, "but I have one last idea that might work."

We huddled for a couple of seconds and I told them what to do. Then we lined up in the form of a triangle.

A whistle blew and the vampire kicker advanced on the ball.

It went high in the air, which I knew would give their kicking team plenty of time to cover us, but the ball came down and I had it in my hands before their advance men reached us.

I stood motionless for a couple of seconds, then I lateraled to Ralph.

Ed and I formed a block for him and he started

119

running toward the empty visitor's side of the field.

I had noticed an open gate over there. I had the feeling that if we could only get off the football field and out of the stadium, we could find the cemetery.

The three of us were now out of bounds on the sidelines. The vampire referees were blowing their whistles.

The vampire football players had stopped because the play had been blown dead, but we continued to run.

Then we heard their terrifying screams, when they realized we had no intentions of stopping and that we were heading toward the open gate, trying to get away.

They had started after us now, I could see.

My leg was throbbing, but I screamed, "Run as hard as you can!"

We had reached the gate now. We ran through it. The stadium lights illuminated what seemed like hundreds of tombstones. *We were inside the cemetery!*

I turned.

The entire vampire football team was coming in waves after us. They were followed by the cheerleaders and the fans from the stands. All their mouths were open and their long, sharp teeth glistened in the stadium lights.

I knew when they reached us we wouldn't have any blood left.

"Find your books and close them!" I shouted to Ralph and Ed. "I'll try to hold off the vampires!"

Ralph and Ed started running toward the rear of the cemetery.

"Come on, Trudy!" I shouted. "Close the book I'm reading!" I covered my neck and face with my arms and fell to the ground.

Then all of a sudden I was lying on the floor in the library.

"You made it!" Trudy cried. "You made it!"

She and Davina were jumping up and down and hugging each other.

Dustin helped the three of us stand up. Davina wanted to change the bandage on my leg, but I wouldn't let her.

"What do we do now?" Anne asked. "Our parents are probably frantic."

"I'm sure they are, but I think we need to take care of another matter first. It means not letting any of your parents know for a couple of hours that you're back, though."

None of the kids who had been inside their books liked the idea, but they agreed to listen to what I had to say.

"We've got to find Ms. Gunkel first. We've got to get to the bottom of this. If we told our parents now what really happened, they'd never believe us, and then Ms. Gunkel would be free to do this at some other elementary school."

"Where do you think she is, Charlie?" Ed asked.

"She's probably at her house. That's where we'll go first."

"What if she comes back to the library while we're trying to find her?" Ralph said. "What if she tries to remove all of these books?"

I hadn't thought about that. "We can't let her do it."

"We could take all the books off the shelves and hide them somewhere," Nancy said.

"We probably need to destroy them," Anne said. "They're terrible."

That was my first thought, too, although I didn't like the idea of destroying books. "Let's wait and see what happens," I said. "Let's just hide them. Trudy, Dustin, Davina, and I will try to find Ms. Gunkel. The five of you stay here and guard the books. Under no circumstances let her remove them."

"We'll make sure nothing happens to them," Bill said.

The four of us started toward the door to the library. I was still limping and my leg hurt a lot, but it made me feel better to know this nightmare was almost over.

For some reason, it seemed darker than I had thought it would be. "What time is it?" I asked.

Trudy looked at her watch. "It's . . . oh, my gosh! It's almost seven o'clock!"

I couldn't believe how much time it had taken to rescue all the kids.

"My parents will be hysterical," Dustin said. "They probably have the police and everyone out looking for me right now."

He was right about that, but we had to solve this problem first.

The halls of the school were pitch black, but I didn't want to turn on any lights.

We began to feel our way along the walls. I knew if we ran into Ms. Gunkel here we were goners. She would be very unhappy that we had rescued all of the Edison Elementary School readers.

Suddenly, we stopped. I had heard a noise at the end of the hall.

"What was that?" I whispered.

"It sounds like someone's trying to open the door," Davina said.

Trudy grabbed my arm. "Do you think it's Ms. Gunkel?"

We listened for a few more minutes, then we realized it was just the wind.

"It's this old building," Dustin said. "The wind comes through all the cracks."

We started walking again.

When we reached the end of the hall, we could see streetlights through the glass door.

We stood there for a few seconds, trying to see if anyone was around who might see us leaving the building.

Finally, I said, "We can't wait any longer. We have to find Ms. Gunkel and confront her."

I pushed the release bar on the door and the four of us stepped out into the night.

The wind was cold.

We ran across the schoolyard to the edge of the street, made two more turns, and then we were on Owl Street.

The wind was howling even more now, blowing the dead leaves off the trees.

Walking as fast as we were, it only took us a few minutes to reach Ms. Gunkel's house.

"What do we do now?" Dustin asked.

I took a deep breath and started up the front porch steps. "I'm not sure, but here goes."

Trudy, Dustin, and Davina followed.

I knocked loudly.

I couldn't hear anyone moving around inside. After a couple of minutes, I tried the door. It opened.

"The candles are still lit," Trudy said.

There seemed to be even more of them, in fact. The coffin we had seen when we first came here was still in the corner of the room. This time I was going to look inside.

I walked over to it slowly. I wasn't sure if it was because my leg was still hurting me or because I was scared.

I pushed the latches at the side of the lid. They snapped open and the sound echoed like thunder through the house.

I looked around fully expecting to see Ms. Gunkel standing in the doorway watching me, but no one appeared.

"Oh, Charlie, let's get out of here," Trudy whispered. "I'm scared."

"Maybe we should leave, Charlie," Dustin said. "We're all back home safely now."

"I have a really bad feeling about all of this," Davina added.

"We can't leave now," I said. "We have to get to the bottom of this." I slowly pushed open the lid of the coffin. There, lying in the middle of the white satin, was a single book: *Write My Name In Blood*.

"A book!" we all cried in unison.

"I just know I saw someone getting out of this coffin the night we came to get the books," I said.

I started toward the kitchen door. "Come on. Ms. Gunkel's probably down in the basement."

Trudy, Dustin, and Davina didn't move. I turned back to them. "You don't have to come if you don't want to. I'll understand."

Trudy swallowed hard. "No. I'm coming. I promised you I'd help you find out what this is all about." She walked over to me.

Dustin and Davina followed.

For some reason, the kitchen seemed much bigger and much darker than it had been when we were first there. It took us forever to reach the door to the basement.

I touched the handle. It felt cold. Wind was coming from through the cracks around the frame.

I turned the knob and the door slammed against me, pinning me to the wall.

Trudy screamed.

"Are you all right, Charlie?" Davina cried.

"No, I'm not all right!" It felt like my nose had been pushed into the back of my head. My eyes were watering from the pain.

The wind coming from the cellar was so strong I could hardly get out from behind the door, and it was only with Dustin's help that I was finally able to.

"We can't go down there," Trudy said.

"We have to!" I shouted above the noise of the wind. I started down the steps, and I was relieved to see that Trudy, Dustin, and Davina were right behind me.

The wind was almost hurricane force now. I had to hold on to the banister with both hands to keep from falling.

The steps seemed to go down and down. I didn't remember that it had taken us this long to reach the cellar the last time we had been there, when we had helped Ms. Gunkel gather up the horror books to put on the shelves of the library.

Down and down we went, and the wind seemed to get stronger and colder. My hands were numb.

Finally, we reached the bottom, and there was Ms. Gunkel, standing beside an open coffin. She was motioning for us to come to her.

"What does she want?" Trudy said.

"We'll soon find out," I said. "Stay behind me and let me do the talking." We started walking slowly over toward where Ms. Gunkel was standing.

When we reached the coffin, the first thing I did was look inside. There was one book lying in the middle. "What's that?" I asked.

"It's a book I want you to read," Ms. Gunkel said. "I think you'll enjoy it a lot. It's very scary."

"I don't want to read any of your books," I said. "I want to know what's going on!"

"Oh, you are so stubborn, Charlie Stanton!" She sighed. "Well, since there's no way for you to escape this time, I guess I can tell you."

I shivered. "What?"

"See that book?" She pointed to the one in the coffin.

I nodded.

"You're looking at a vampire."

"A *vampire?*"

"Yes. People have this strange notion that all vampires look like Dracula. Well, they don't. Vampires can take all kinds of shapes. These particular vampires are horror books."

"You mean all vampires don't wear black capes and have fangs and suck blood out of your neck?"

"No, not all. Some do, of course—probably the vast majority, in fact—but these particular vampires become horror books and feed on the whole body of the reader. They pull you into their story and you become a character. When they've fed on a certain number of young readers, they become duplicate copies. This is how they multiply. You can't even begin to imagine how many readers they must devour to become best-sellers."

"Well, why do you have to become characters in them? Why can't you just read them for fun?"

129

"Charlie! Charlie! The vampires have to be fed in order to survive."

I looked around. "Why are you telling me this, anyway?" I was trying to put on a brave front. "As soon as we leave here we're going to tell everybody, and you'll really be in trouble then."

"But you're not going to leave here, Charlie. You'll never get away now. All four of you are going to read these new books, and this time there will be no one to close them before you've finished!"

"You won't get away with this!" I shouted at her.

"Oh, yes, I will. You have no idea how many young readers are now characters in the books they read. Thousands and thousands." She sighed. "You were just lucky. It never occurred to me that you wouldn't be holding the book in your hand when you were reading it, that it would just be lying on the table. Most people hold books in their hands when they read them, Charlie. Why did you have to be so different?"

The wind continued to howl. It was bitterly cold.

"I won't do it!" I cried. "*We* won't do it. We won't read any book you try to get us to read."

Ms. Gunkel acted as though she hadn't heard

a word I said. She reached into four different coffins and picked up four different books.

"What are we going to do, Charlie?" Trudy whispered.

"I say we make a run for it!" Dustin said.

"We can do it, Charlie," Davina said.

I looked back at the open door we had come through. It seemed really far away, but I thought we could make it.

Then it suddenly slammed shut.

Ms. Gunkel started laughing. "You can't get away, if that's what you're thinking. The vampires have to be fed." She handed each of us a book. "Start reading!"

"No!" I cried. I threw my book down on the ground. Trudy, Dustin, and Davina did the same. "You can't make us do it!" There had to be another way out of here, I thought. There just had to be!

I grabbed Trudy's hand. "Come on!" I started pulling her through the darkness, dragging my leg behind me. Dustin and Davina were right behind us.

"You'll never get away! You're under the Duncanville Cemetery," Ms. Gunkel screamed. "There is no escape!"

"You mean her cellar really is *under* the cemetery?" Trudy cried.

131

"It looks like it," I said.

There were coffins everywhere. Each one had several candles on the lid. Tree roots were hanging down from the ground above, making it hard to run, and bats were flying all around us.

Behind us, Ms. Gunkel continued to laugh. "You'll get bored after a while running around in circles!" she shouted. "You'll want to read a book just to escape!" She laughed some more.

"No way!" Dustin shouted back at her.

The tree roots were getting thicker and thicker and kept lashing at our faces like whips.

"I think we're in the new part of the cemetery," I said, "because there are more trees in that part."

Suddenly, I looked up and I could see the moon. "This is it!" I cried.

"What?" Trudy said.

"I know how we can get out!"

"I'm coming to get you," Ms. Gunkel cried. "It's time to read!"

"We're under an open grave," I said. "They must have just finished digging it. There's no coffin here."

The three of them looked up.

"I can see the moon, too," Davina said.

"Here! Grab one of these tree roots and start climbing!"

132

"I don't think I can," Trudy said.

"I'm coming!" Ms. Gunkel called.

"Maybe I can!" Trudy added hurriedly.

Each one of us grabbed a tree root and started climbing toward the open grave. Dustin was halfway up when his broke.

He fell to the ground with a thud.

"You'll never get away!" Ms. Gunkel said. "You'll never . . . What are you doing?" She gave a high-pitched shriek. "Stop it! Stop it! The vampires have to be fed!"

I could hear her feet thudding on the ground. Now she was running toward us.

"Dustin? Grab another one! Quick!"

Trudy and Davina were gasping for breath. I wasn't sure they were going to make it.

Dustin grabbed another tree root and started climbing as fast as he could.

Ms. Gunkel had reached us now and was shaking her fists and jumping up and down. "An open grave!" she screamed. "Oh, an open grave!" Then she grabbed the tree root I was climbing and started swinging it. I was going around in circles. I just knew it was going to break any minute, but I kept climbing.

Now I was even with Trudy and Davina.

Trudy had her eyes closed. "I can't make it, Charlie!" she sobbed. "I can't make it!"

133

"Yes, you can!" Davina told her. "We're almost to the opening of the grave!"

I wasn't sure I was going to make it, though, because the tree root I was climbing was swinging so violently. Then it stopped, and Ms. Gunkel started swinging the one that Trudy was on.

Trudy screamed.

I grabbed her waist and pulled to her mine because it was thicker. "Hold on!" I whispered.

She had her arms around my waist, but I could feel her slipping.

I was pulling with all my might.

"I can feel the grass on the top of the grave, Charlie!" Dustin cried.

I looked over and saw him pulling himself out. Davina was climbing out right behind him. It seemed like it took them forever, but finally they were all the way out. Dustin reached down and I grabbed his hand. Davina grabbed Trudy's and together they pulled us out.

Suddenly, all around us there were high-pitched screams and the sounds of people running away.

"What was that all about?" I said, as I lay panting on the ground beside the open grave.

"Vandals, probably," Dustin said. "They must have been planning to knock over some of the tombstones here in the cemetery."

We all started laughing.

I could just picture what they must have thought when they saw the four of us climbing out of the empty grave.

I finally forced myself to sit up.

"We have to get back to the library," Trudy said. "We have to destroy those books!"

I still didn't like the idea of destroying books, but these really weren't books. They were vampires! If they didn't feed on readers, then what would happen to them? I wondered.

We all stood up and started running toward the entrance to the cemetery. I could feel blood trickling down from the wound on my leg.

"I just hope we can get back to the library before Ms. Gunkel does," Trudy said.

"I just hope she doesn't see us when we run by in front of her house," Dustin said.

We finally reached the entrance to the cemetery and raced past Ms. Gunkel's house.

She was nowhere around that we could see.

We ran the five blocks down Owl Street to where it intersected the street that led to the school.

When we got to the school building, I tried the front door, but it was locked. So was the back door.

"You didn't think they'd be open, did you?" Trudy said.

I really hadn't, but I was hoping. "We'll just have to knock on the windows of the library and hope that someone will look out and see us."

It took several tries before Anne's face appeared.

"Open the back door!" I cried. "We've got to destroy those books!"

We ran to the back of the school and waited.

Finally, Bill and Anne opened the door. "What happened? Did you find Ms. Gunkel?"

"Yes," I said, hurrying past them and racing down the dark hallway. "Are the books still in the library?"

Bill was right behind me. "They should be. We didn't do anything except hide them."

We had reached the library now.

I opened the door and turned on all the overhead lights. Then Bill took me to where they had hidden all of the horror books that Ms. Gunkel had put on the shelves.

I stopped and stared. They were no longer books. They were just piles of red dust.

Everyone was looking at the piles of red dust with stunned expressions.

"How could that have happened?" Anne said.

"We never left the library," Nancy said.

"It wouldn't have made any difference. It happened because none of us stayed inside them," I said. "The vampires had nothing to feed upon, so they turned to dust."

They all looked at me.

"What are you talking about, Charlie?" Bill asked.

I sighed. "I'll tell you on the way to see our parents." I turned and started out of the library. "Come on."

We made up a story about getting locked in the basement of the school. That was believable because over the years the basement had been the source of all kinds of horror stories.

137

We knew we'd be punished by our parents and by the school authorities, but we decided that would be better than telling them what really happened because no one would believe us.

I had a harder time explaining the bite marks on my leg. My story about a huge rat worked, but it landed me in the hospital for the rest of the week, where I had to suffer through a series of rabies shots.

The next Saturday afternoon, Trudy, Dustin, Davina, and I walked back down Owl Street to Ms. Gunkel's house. It was all boarded up.

"I heard she called Mr. Scoville and told him she had to leave town because of a family emergency," Trudy said.

"Yeah! A family of *vampires!*" I said.

"I wonder if the rest of her books turned to dust like the ones in the library," Dustin said.

"I doubt it," Davina said. "She's probably on her way to some other unsuspecting elementary school to make sure they don't."

"Maybe we should tell somebody about this after all," Trudy said.

I looked at her. "Do you honestly think anyone would believe us?"

They all agreed that no one would, so we decided just to take whatever punishment we were given.

Monday, when I went back to school, my only punishment was no recess for the entire week. Everyone else had already suffered the consequences. I was, however, allowed to go to the library and read.

I wasn't quite sure I ever wanted to pick up another horror book in my entire life, but I knew I wouldn't have to worry about that now because Mrs. Hart was back and there wouldn't be any horror books on the library shelves.

So you can imagine my surprise when Mrs. Hart said, "While I was in the hospital, Charlie, I thought a lot about you."

"You did?"

She nodded. "Yes, I did. I've been wrong not letting you read what you want to read. There's nothing wrong with horror books. Nothing at all."

"There isn't?" I managed to say.

Mrs. Hart had a big grin on her face. "No. Absolutely not." Then she brought out a book from behind her back. "Look what I have for you! I found it on a shelf in the storage room. I'm not quite sure how it got there, but it doesn't matter." She held it out for me to take. "Here. Start reading."

Uh, oh! I thought. We missed one. "I don't think I should, Mrs. Hart," I said. "I know how you really feel about horror books. Maybe you're right after all."

"Nonsense!" Mrs. Hart continued to smile. "I've changed my mind. Now, take it and start reading."

I didn't seem to have a choice. Had Ms. Gunkel somehow talked Mrs. Hart into getting even with me? I wondered. I took the book. It was called *My Parents Are Werewolves*. I opened it to the first page. Then I looked up. "Maybe I'll take it home and read it later."

"Read it now," Mrs. Hart said. She still had that smile on her face.

I started reading.

I read all the way through the first page. Nothing happened.

Maybe I was just being paranoid about this whole thing after all. Maybe Mrs. Hart really had decided there was nothing wrong with our reading horror books during library period. "It's good," I said. "It's really good."

"Well, I'm glad. Now you just go over to that table and read to your heart's content."

I did as I was told, but when I got to the table I laid the book close to the edge so that if anyone bumped against it, it would fall off and close. After all I'd been through, I decided, there was no sense in taking any more chances.

I started reading the book again.

But I had only read a couple of pages when I reached down to scratch at the bandage on my leg. The werewolf bite was itching like crazy!

That's when I noticed my hands. They had thick brown hair all over them and were beginning to look like ... *paws.*

Alexander was nervous. He glanced around the classroom. It looked like something out of an old movie. The windows were tall and narrow, and an old-fashioned coatrack stood beside the door. The floors were pale wood, scarred and stained, and the desks looked like beat-up garage sale antiques. At the back of the classroom, shelves were filled with faded, dusty books. In front, a giant old-fashioned blackboard was decorated with two dusty portraits. One was of Abraham Lincoln, the other George Washington. Both were frowning. Alexander swallowed. This was going to be awful.

Alexander realized that the teacher was talking to him. He tried to concentrate on what she was saying.

"Will you help Mr. Gleason bring up your desk?" Mrs. Ament asked. Alexander nodded, startled out of his thoughts. She gestured and

Alexander saw a white-haired man standing in the doorway. He had on gray pants and an olive-green shirt. "Mr. Gleason is our janitor," Mrs. Ament said, making it a formal introduction. "This is our newest student, Alexander Hanifin."

Alexander stepped forward when Mr. Gleason extended his hand. The old man's skin was papery and ridged with veins, but his grip was strong. When he turned, Alexander followed, grateful to walk away from the curious stares.

Mr. Gleason led him out of the classroom into the little entry hall, where Alexander had hung his coat along with everyone else. A small window in the door on the opposite side gave Alexander a glimpse of another classroom.

"That's fifth and sixth, Mrs. Schack's room. First and second grades are downstairs with Mrs. Fredericksen," Mr. Gleason said, watching him. "The cafeteria is downstairs, too. But we're going to the basement." He gestured to the hanging coats. "You might want to get your jacket. There's an indoor stairway, but it's in Mrs. Schack's classroom and I don't want to disturb them. So we'll do it the hard way." He nodded toward the heavy double doors that led outside.

Alexander pulled down his jacket and slid it on as he followed Mr. Gleason out into the cold autumn air. The small red brick school had been

146

built on the edge of a huge wheat field. The playground was surrounded by towering cottonwood trees, bare and gray against the sky. As he and Mr. Gleason rounded the corner of the school, a wind rattled through the branches, scattering dead leaves along the ground.

"It's down there," Mr. Gleason said, stopping in front of a pair of white wooden doors. He fiddled with the ring of keys hanging from his belt. "These stairs," he warned Alexander as he opened the padlock, "are very steep. You watch your step."

Alexander nodded and swallowed, but he wasn't really listening. In five minutes or less he was going to be sitting in that musty old classroom. He didn't know anyone, he didn't like Jordan's uneasy friendliness and he was already afraid of the mean-looking kid. For a second, he wished desperately that his family had never moved to Littleton. But once his father got an idea, no one could talk him out of it.

"Here we go," Mr. Gleason said, leaning in to switch on a light. He started down the stairs. Alexander waited a second before following.

The stairs were unbelievably steep. There was a handrail of smooth gray metal, obviously added years after the basement had been built, but it was so low that it was awkward to use. The musty smell Alexander had noticed in the class-room was stronger here, thicker with every step downward—and the stairs seemed to go on forever. Then, finally, Mr. Gleason paused and turned. "Make it okay?"

Alexander nodded, looking around. A single bare light bulb hanging from the middle of the ceiling cast a tangle of ink-dark shadows on all four walls. It was a big room and every corner of it was full. There were tables and folding chairs neatly stacked at the front of the storeroom, and Mr. Gleason had kept an aisle clear so that they could be brought in and out. The rest of the room was a jumble. Rolled maps leaned at crazy angles and boxes were piled precariously, some of them tipping so far it was amazing they hadn't fallen. Mr. Gleason made his way slowly forward, humming a little. He patted a desk as he passed it. "This one is broken. But there's one over here."

"Don't you know where the new desks are?" Alexander asked, startled, then realized it sounded rude. Before he could apologize, Mr. Gleason laughed quietly.

"You'd think so, wouldn't you? But we don't often need an extra desk, so the school board doesn't buy us any new ones. Usually, there's a spare in one of the other classrooms." He slid some boxes to one side, still talking. "This year, we've had five new students. The area's growing."

Alexander nodded. That was what his father kept saying. That was why they'd moved here. His father wanted to build a subdivision. He was convinced the city was expanding this way.

"There's one back here, I think," Mr. Gleason was saying. Alexander nodded and waited while Mr. Gleason poked and pushed his way through more piles of dusty school supplies. Alexander lifted the flap of a box and looked inside. There were textbooks that looked like they belonged in a museum.

"Here," Mr. Gleason said, startling him. "Can you give me a hand, son?"

Alexander waded into the maze of junk. Mr. Gleason was shoving a stack of boxes to one side. "Here. It's a little beat up, but it's sturdy enough."

Alexander lifted the front part of the desk and together he and Mr. Gleason carried it toward the stairs, zigzagging around boxes and piles of paper supplies. Once they had cleared the last stack of boxes, Mr. Gleason stopped. "Let's set it down for a second."

Alexander bent to ease the desk to the floor. Mr. Gleason straightened and pulled a rag from his back pocket. "Look at this now."

Alexander blinked. In the harsh light of the bare light bulb, letters carved into the desk top stood out. Alexander ran his fingers over them. "Simon," he read aloud. He looked up at Mr. Gleason.

Mr. Gleason winked. "One of the bad boys. They used to make them come down here, you know. Sit in the dark for an hour."

Alexander shivered, imagining sitting here while someone closed the heavy doors at the top of the stairs, then being alone in the dark. Mr. Gleason reached out to squeeze his shoulder. "I'll bet it was awful. Only made the kids angrier and worse. Now we all know better." Mr. Gleason ran the rag over the rest of the desk, shook the rag out, then wiped it again. Then he cleared his throat. "All right. Let's see if we can lug this thing up those steps." He tucked the rag back in his pocket and nodded briskly. "It'll be easier for you to go up first. I'd have to bend in half."

Alexander nodded, more than ready to get out of the stuffy storeroom and back into the daylight. He gripped the edge of the desk and started up the stairs backwards. Mr. Gleason lifted his side high so that Alexander didn't have to stoop too far.

They stopped twice to adjust their holds and for a few seconds' rest. Finally, Alexander stepped

150

onto level ground and walked backward a few steps more. The wind had picked up and the air had gotten colder. He could hear the cottonwoods creaking as they swayed.

"Set it down, son," Mr. Gleason instructed. "I can get it from here."

Alexander let the weight of the desk down slowly. As he released it, he impulsively ran his hands over the name carved into the wood. An odd heat burned his fingers. He jumped back, startled.

"You okay?" Mr. Gleason looked concerned. "This wasn't too heavy for you, was it?"

Alexander shook his head, puzzled and embarrassed. He was so nervous he was imagining things. He looked up at the sky. There were dark clouds on the horizon. Maybe it was going to storm.

"Let's get you back to class," Mr. Gleason said. Alexander nodded. The first day was always the worst at a new school. He might as well get it over with. He touched the faded oak desk lightly, proving to himself that he'd imagined the feeling of heat. Mr. Gleason hoisted the desk up and slowly led the way.